Seven Interviews

Mark Dunn

A SAMUEL FRENCH ACTING EDITION

SAMUEL
FRENCH
FOUNDED 1830

SAMUELFRENCH.COM
SAMUELFRENCH-LONDON.CO.UK

ISBN 978-0-573-70215-0

www.SamuelFrench.com
www.SamuelFrench-London.co.uk

MUSIC USE NOTE

Licensees are solely responsible for obtaining formal written permission from copyright owners to use copyrighted music in the performance of this play and are strongly cautioned to do so. If no such permission is obtained by the licensee, then the licensee must use only original music that the licensee owns and controls. Licensees are solely responsible and liable for all music clearances and shall indemnify the copyright owners of the play(s) and their licensing agent, Samuel French, against any costs, expenses, losses and liabilities arising from the use of music by licensees. Please contact the appropriate music licensing authority in your territory for the rights to any incidental music.

IMPORTANT BILLING AND CREDIT REQUIREMENTS

If you have obtained performance rights to this title, please refer to your licensing agreement for important billing and credit requirements.

SEVEN INTERVIEWS opened at Auxiliary Dog Theatre in Albuquerque, New Mexico on September 11, 2009. It was mounted as a Ka-HOOTZ Theatre Company "Emerging Directors' Project." The producer was Lou Clark, and the directing mentors were Susan Pearson and Denise Schulz. The stage manager was Kathleen Richardson. The lighting design was by David Rogulich. The sound design was by Kevin McGuire.

The pieces were directed by Joanna Furgal, Maggz Gallegos, Bradd Howard, Nick Lopez, Lauren Myers, and Kathleen Richardson.

Featured in the acting ensemble were David Bommarito, Lou Clark, Becca Holmes, Nick Lopez, Paul Middleton, Ninette S. Mordaunt, Hal Simons, and Tawni Waters.

CHARACTERS

ACTOR

The First Interview: **ROGER TODDLE** – 50s; a thin veneer of business-like professionalism overlaying a chewy center of pure terror and hysteria.

The Third Interview: **GORDON GREEN** – mid 50s; affable, good-natured, enjoying the new-found freedom of his early retirement.

The Fourth Interview: **FRANK HALLOWELL** – late 40s; begrudging but not belligerent, still learning the new language of his predicament.

The Fifth Interview: **HUCK GLEASON** – early 50s; good-hearted, spiritually grounded farmer, who loves his daughter and grandson intensely.

The Sixth Interview: **VINCENT GAMPION** – late 40s; slick, no-nonsense professional criminal with none of the color and cartoonery of a TV gangster.

The Seventh Interview: **ABEL MARCH** – early 50s; fairly unlikeable at first, distracted, distraught, revealing his humanity belatedly.

YOUNGER ACTRESS

The First Interview: **GINA GALLAGHER** – early 30s; politeness and propriety that disintegrates into a major flight reflex.

The Second Interview: **DELORES CARR** – 30s; self-important, takes herself and her task far too seriously.

The Fourth Interview: **YVONNE SIMS** – 30s; head-on-straight, comfortable in her skin.

The Fifth Interview: **DEANNE SPRAWLEY** – late 20s; a woman wrestling with her faith, angry, mournful, and worn to a frazzle.

The Sixth Interview: **JULIANNA BUCHNER** – 30s; a mother in deep torment, laser-focused on her retaliatory mission.

The Seventh Interview: **BRITTNEY FLETCHER** – early 20s; beautiful, sexy, trashy, selfish and very hungry.

OLDER ACTRESS

The First Interview: **BEATRICE CARPENTER** – 40s; happy, adaptive, always good-naturedly clueless.

The Second Interview: **TIMOTHINA RUSSELL** – 50s; colorful? eccentric? outright insane?

The Third Interview: **FELICIA PENETTI** – late 40s; proper and by-the-book, a self-starter, yet quite affable.

The *Fourth Interview:* **DR. JUDY GABLE** – late 40s; a straight-laced psychologist, sure-footed, egotistical, before she becomes a bowl of emotional jelly.

The Fifth Interview: **MYRA HENDERSON** – 40s; more than just a religious prig; strongly principled; one who struggles with confrontations.

The Seventh Interview: **MS. DOMANIAN** – late 40s; a circumstantial thief with a golden heart, grandmotherly, old-worldly.

There will be an offstage female voice heard through an intercom in the Fourth Interview.

SETTING

All of the interviews take place in the United States. Although some of the dialogue may feel more suitable to specific parts of the country (The Fifth Interview, for example, has a southern feel. The Sixth Interview seems more appropriate to the urban Northeast.), producers are free to place these offices wherever they see fit.

TIME

The Seven Interviews take place in the not-too-distant past, the present, and the near future.

AUTHOR'S NOTES

Seven Interviews is comprised of seven very different two- and three-person interviews. While ostensibly a series of twelve-to-twenty-five-minute-long-playlets, each of which could easily stand on its own, they work best when produced together as a cohesive unit. *Seven Interviews* is intended as a vehicle for three versatile actors – two women and one man – each of whom will be called upon to play six very different characters. The man should be able to play male characters in their late forties to early sixties. The first woman should be able to play female characters in their twenties and early thirties, and the second woman, female characters in their forties and early fifties. However, the author would have no objection to the casting of these roles (eighteen in all) with as many actors as suits the needs of a particular production. Since he envisions *Seven Interviews* as a good vehicle for showcasing the work of directing and acting students in high schools and colleges, latitude may also be taken in assigning ages to the characters. (A list of suggested character assignments for a three-actor production precedes this page.)

Simplicity of staging will also serve the production well. All that is required in terms of set pieces is a desk and sometimes two, sometimes three chairs. Should it be the desire of the designer to, say, fit a multi-level stage with several desks and chairs of various sizes and descriptions, this would likewise be permissible.

Basically, anything goes, so long as the presentation remains simple and elemental. *Seven Interviews* is, at its core, a collection of seven needful conversations in an interview format, all of which are ultimately transforming, and all driven by the colloquy itself.

An intermission is recommended between interviews four and five.

Mark Dunn

*Seven Interviews is dedicated to four individuals who
brightened my Albuquerque sojourn with their friendship,
support and talent:
Ninette Mordaunt, Joel Miller, Hugh Witemeyer, and V.J. Liberatori*

The First Interview

ROGER TODDLE

GINA GALLAGHER

BEATRICE CARPENTER

(Lights come up on the office of **ROGER TODDLE**. *He stands in front of his desk, greeting* **GINA GALLAGHER**, *who has just arrived. Note that the desk has all the normal office accouterments, including a laptop computer and telephone. The same desk setup, with only slight variations, can be used for all seven interviews.)*

TODDLE. Did you have any trouble finding the building? We're a little tucked away back here. Some people miss us.

GINA. No, your directions were perfect.

TODDLE. Fine. Fine. Have a seat.

(The two take their seats, **TODDLE** *behind the desk,* **GINA** *in front of it.)*

The employment agency gave you all the particulars?

GINA. *(nodding)* They said the job was for secretary and office receptionist.

TODDLE. That's right. You'd be my girl Friday. Do you know what my company – Main Street Solutions – do you know what it is that we *do*, Ms. Gallagher?

GINA. You're a consulting business.

TODDLE. *(nodding)* We advise small businessmen.

(quickly correcting himself)

Owners of small businesses.

GINA. I knew what you meant.

TODDLE. I didn't mean – you know – "Little People."

GINA. Of course not. Although I'm sure you wouldn't exclude them.

TODDLE. Oh no, no, no.

(beat)

And women.

GINA. I beg your pardon?

TODDLE. Female business owners too. I said "business*men*" but what I meant was –

GINA. Yes, I understood, Mr. Toddle. Is everything all right, Mr. Toddle?

TODDLE. I'm fine. I'm a little warm.

(He takes a moment to collect himself, then launches into his spiel.)

Main Street Solutions offers strategies for making businesses run better. We help companies find avenues for growth financing. I'm a creature of the banking world, Ms. Gallagher. Everything comes down to capital investment. Finding money to *make* money. So before I begin with *my* questions, is there anything you'd like to ask *me?*

GINA. *(caught a little off-guard)* Oh. All right. Um. How quickly would you need your new secretary to start? Because it looks like you don't have one. I mean, there was nobody sitting at your secretary's desk out there, and there was, you know, no, um, coat hanging on the rack.

TODDLE. You're very observant, Ms. Gallagher. But your eyes have deceived you. I still have a secretary. I sent her off on an errand so I could conduct this interview without her being here.

GINA. Oh. So when will she be leaving?

TODDLE. Soon. Quite soon.

GINA. You don't have an exact date for when you'd like to have a new person in that position?

TODDLE. It's all a little fluid right now.

GINA. What does that mean?

TODDLE. It means that I haven't fired her yet.

(a silence, as **GINA** *digests this important fact)*

But it's coming. Any day now.

GINA. Any day now.

TODDLE. Could be tomorrow, in fact.

GINA. Because she isn't working out.

TODDLE. That's right. She isn't working out so I need a replacement secretary.

GINA. May I ask how long your present secretary has been with you?

TODDLE. Of course you may.

(adding it up in his head)

Ms. Carpenter has been in my employ seven – no – eight years, as of May. I remember that I hired her right after Mother's Day ... eight years ago.

GINA. Oh. Well, I suppose it's none of my – Mr. Toddle, eight years is a long time.

TODDLE. *(nodding)* It is. It is. They were good years. She's been a good secretary. I just don't want her to *be* my secretary any more. Now, may I take the reins of this interview? I mean if you're done with your questions.

*(***GINA*** *nods, noticeably uneasy.* ***TODDLE*** *picks up what we assume to be* ***GINA****'s résumé and looks it over.)*

You're a little over qualified.

GINA. Is that a problem?

TODDLE. You have a Bachelor's Degree.

GINA. In English lit. I thought I wanted to teach. Then I decided I *didn't* want to teach. I've always fantasized about some day running my own business, so yours is just the kind of company that –

(interrupting herself with a different train of thought)

Mr. Toddle, I'm sorry, but do you really think it's such a good idea: interviewing possible replacements for your secretary when she doesn't even know she's about to lose her job?

TODDLE. Now that really shouldn't be any concern of yours, Ms. Gallagher.

GINA. When were you going to tell her?

TODDLE. As soon as I hired a new secretary. Now may I –

GINA. What if she comes back here too early and catches me? She'll wonder who I am.

TODDLE. I sent her all the way across town, Ms. Gallagher. She isn't coming back for quite some time.

GINA. It just doesn't feel right to me.

TODDLE. Well, I'm sorry if you –

GINA. *(interrupting)* And besides, Mr. Toddle, the employment agency didn't say that I'd be interviewing for a position that wasn't even available yet.

TODDLE. You're right. I wasn't up front with the agency. In fact, I lied. To be honest with you, Ms. Gallagher, I'm dreading having to fire her. But it has to be done. I just have to find the right time – do it under the proper circumstances. Her sister's been visiting from out of town and then there was Thanksgiving last week, and I'm really not a bad person, Ms. Gallagher. It's just that I can't work with her anymore.

GINA. What's wrong with her?

TODDLE. *(hedging)* Now Ms. Gallagher, it wouldn't be right for me to –

GINA. But how will I know if I'm prone to make the same mistakes *she* did?

TODDLE. She didn't make mistakes. It isn't about mistakes.

(an uncomfortable silence)

I apologize, Ms. Gallagher. Things have gotten a little off track, and I'm very sorry.

GINA. You don't have to –

TODDLE. Look, I'm really a very nice person. You would come to realize this once you got to know me.

(changes course)

This is very difficult for me, Ms. Gallagher.

GINA. You mean the fact that you have to fire your present secretary? Or are you talking about the *reason* she has to go?

TODDLE. Well, *everything*, really. We've spent – as I said –

TODDLE & GINA. *(together)* Eight years...

TODDLE. ...together. Yes. I mean, there are a lot of *marriages* that don't last that long. But you see, and I'll just put it out there, Ms. Gallagher, because I am nothing if not an honest broker. That's why my consulting business has done so well – I just tell people the truth and they appreciate the fact that I'm –

TODDLE & GINA. *(together)* Up front...

TODDLE. ...with them. Yes.

(his voice taking on a confidential tone)

You see: here's the thing. She gives me nightmares.

GINA. Nightmares.

TODDLE. Yes.

GINA. You mean literal, middle-of-the-night nightmares?

TODDLE. That's right. Ms. Carpenter gives me nightmares. It's not something I'm proud to admit. I've told a couple of people. I've told my doctor.

GINA. Your psychiatrist?

TODDLE. No. My family doctor. I've told my family doctor, because I haven't been sleeping well, and he wanted to know why I wasn't sleeping well and so I told him that I've been having nightmares about my secretary.

GINA. Was he the one who suggested you let her go?

TODDLE. Of course not. To be honest, Ms. Gallagher, I would prefer *not* to have to let her go, but the nightmares aren't going away, and I'm a zombie without a good night's rest and this situation has become intolerable. So there's the story. And I've told you much more than I should have. I hope that the other applicants don't make me. The whole thing is quite embarrassing.

GINA. Of course you have yet to tell me *why* she gives you nightmares.

TODDLE. Please don't make me think about it, Ms. Gallagher.

(suddenly jumps, recoils, listens)

Did you hear that?

GINA. Hear what?

(He bounces up and goes to an implied window.)

TODDLE. Oh God!

GINA. What is it?

TODDLE. It's *her*. She's back already. She couldn't possibly have driven all the way across town and gotten back here this quickly.

GINA. Where did you send her?

TODDLE. Manny's. The men's clothing store. I told her I needed a new braided black belt. The dog chewed up my last one. I sent her to Manny's. It's way over by the airport.

GINA. There's a new Manny's. It just opened on Elm Street not too far from here.

TODDLE. *(thrown into a sudden panic)* Elm Street? There's a new Manny's on *Elm Street?*

GINA. The ads were all over the TV. You didn't see the one with the horse wearing the bow tie?

TODDLE. *(looking out the window, panicked)* I didn't see the horse. I never saw the horse. Oh God, oh God. She's getting out of the car. She's got my belt. She's such a damned good secretary. Look how quickly she got that belt.

GINA. I think I'd better go.

(She gets up and starts out of the office in the direction from which she entered.)

TODDLE. Oh no no no no no – you can't go out *that* way!

GINA. Is there another way?

TODDLE. Here. Climb out the window.

GINA. What?

TODDLE. The window. Climb out the window.

GINA. Mr. Toddle, are you insane?

TODDLE. Yes, I'm insane. This whole thing has made me certifiable. You shouldn't be going. You should be staying. I need to do this. I need to fire her. Sit down. I need a witness.

GINA. Mr. Toddle, I'm not comfortable with this.

TODDLE. What if I hire you right now, right on the spot? What if I do *that?*

GINA. Mr. Toddle, I'm not sure I even want this job.

TODDLE. Of course you do. And I'm almost positive *you* won't give me nightmares.

(stiffens up, closes his eyes, listening)

She's in. She's hanging up her coat. Just like in the nightmares. She puts her coat on a peg and then she puts her purse in her desk and then she opens the door and there it is.

GINA. There *what* is?

*(**TODDLE** doesn't have time to answer. **BEATRICE** enters. **BEATRICE** wears a very large black eye patch. The sight of it gives **GINA** a little start. **BEATRICE** carries a small shopping bag that says "Manny's.")*

BEATRICE. I'm sorry, Mr. Toddle. I didn't know you had someone in your office.

TODDLE. *(trying his best to hold it together)* That's quite all right, Ms. Carpenter. I see you got the belt.

BEATRICE. It's a very nice store. I was going to get my brother something for his birthday while I was there, but I knew you wouldn't want me to dawdle.

*(extending her hand to shake **GINA**'s)*

Hello. I'm Mr. Toddle's secretary, Beatrice Carpenter. And you are – ?

GINA. Gina Gallagher.

(*They shake.*)

BEATRICE. So nice to meet you. Are you hiring us?

GINA. I beg your pardon?

BEATRICE. Established business or start-up?

GINA. (*obviously lost as to how to answer*) I don't –

TODDLE. Ms. Gallagher isn't a potential client, Ms. Carpenter.

BEATRICE. Oh.

(*apparently thinking she's figured it out; with a nod and a smile.*)

Ohhhhh.

GINA. *Ohhhhh* what?

BEATRICE. (*to* **GINA**) Mr. Toddle has started dating again. How nice. Take her to the new steak place on Oakdale, Mr. Toddle. It's quite lovely and very romantic… I mean, for a steakhouse.

(**BEATRICE** *takes a pencil from* **TODDLE**'*s desk.*)

TODDLE. Thank you, Ms. Carpenter, but I'm not –

(**BEATRICE** *lifts her eye patch slightly to scratch underneath it with the pencil.* **TODDLE** *shudders.*)

TODDLE. (*turning away in horror*) What are you doing? What are you doing, Ms. Carpenter?

BEATRICE. The socket itches.

TODDLE. Could you do that somewhere else, please?

BEATRICE. Certainly. Here's your belt, Mr. Toddle. The receipt's in the bag and you can just pay me whenever you want. I put it on my credit card.

(*handing* **TODDLE** *the bag*)

And it was so nice to meet you, Ms. Gallagher.

(*She starts to put the pencil back on the desk, but then, apparently thinking better of it, switches it to the other hand so she can shake* **GINA**'*s hand again.*)

BEATRICE. *(cont.)* I hope I'll be seeing more of you.

GINA. *(ill at ease)* Yes, thank you.

(**BEATRICE** *goes. There is a short silence.*)

Is that it?

(**TODDLE** *nods.*)

How did she – ?

TODDLE. She's never told me. And I've never asked. Three weeks ago – a Monday morning – she walks in wearing the eye patch.

GINA. Could it be some kind of affectation? I mean, she mentioned "socket" but maybe she was kidding. Maybe she's got a fully-functioning eyeball under there.

TODDLE. *(considering this)* An affectation.

GINA. Like she's chosen to wear the patch as, you know, a kind of – um – *accessory.*

TODDLE. I never thought about that. Now that would be very odd.

GINA. Yes. But perhaps she might take off the patch – end the affectation – if you asked her to. Especially if she knew that it would mean the difference between keeping her job and losing it.

TODDLE. You have a point. Now how would I go about asking her such a thing?

GINA. Well, you just have to come right out and ask her. You can't beat around the bush with something like that.

TODDLE. So, okay, I just…

GINA. …ask her. That's right.

TODDLE. And just how would *you* put it? I mean, if it were you?

GINA. I would simply say: "Ms. Carpenter, I was wondering how you lost your eye, if, that is, you feel like telling me." I'd be – um – very polite about it – you know, give her the benefit of the doubt that unfortunate circumstances have put her in this situation.

TODDLE. *(brightening)* And that she isn't just wearing that eye patch to give me night sweats.

(GINA nods.)

That's very good.

(beat)

You're very good. Perhaps *you* should be the one to ask her.

GINA. Me?

TODDLE. Yes. You're the perfect person to do it. I mean let us just assume that you *are* my new girlfriend. Who's to say that you aren't by nature a very frank and forthcoming kind of person, and it's your candor that I fell in love with?

GINA. I suppose that would work. Of course, at some point you'd have to tell her that I'm *not* your girlfriend, and then what are you going to say that I am? I mean, assuming that she's willing to remove the eye patch to keep her job?

TODDLE. Why don't we cross that bridge when we come to it?

(He picks up phone handset and speaks into it.)

Ms. Carpenter? Could you step in here please?

(A moment passes. BEATRICE enters.)

(nervously) My girlfriend has a question she'd like to ask you, Ms. Carpenter. Ask away, Gina, my girlfriend.

GINA. *(caught off-guard)* Oh. All right. I was just wondering, Ms. Carpenter – because I'm a nosy sort of person…

TODDLE. *(interjecting)* She's very nosy, very curious. That's one of the things I like about her.

GINA. …how you came to lose your eye.

BEATRICE. How sweet of you to ask. It was a freak accident. During my vacation last month. I found myself in the path of a stray tranquilizer dart at the Wild African safari. It's next to Epcot. I was just sitting in the car and wham! Suddenly, I have one less working eyeball and one hell of a personal injury lawsuit. It just falls right into my lap. The lawsuit. Not the eye.

(to **TODDLE***)*

I was going to tell you before the end of the day, Mr. Toddle, but this seems just as good a time as any. The settlement check arrived yesterday from the lawyers with the animal park, and it's very generous. So I don't need to work here anymore. This is my two-week notice.

(to **GINA** *who is still staring at the eye patch)*

Do you like it? It's very stylish. And quite soft. It's velour on the inside. Feel that nap.

(With her back to the audience but in full view of **TODDLE**, **BEATRICE** *pulls up the eye patch to show the inside lining to* **GINA**, *who quails.* **TODDLE** *squeals in fear.* **BEATRICE** *quickly pulls the patch back down into place.)*

BEATRICE. *(cont.)* Are you all right, Mr. Toddle? Sit down, Mr. Toddle. I'll get you a glass of water.

(She dashes out of the room.)

TODDLE. *(to himself)* They'll never stop now. Every night. Until I'm dead.

GINA. I have to go.

TODDLE. Don't go. I need you.

GINA. I've decided that I don't want the job.

TODDLE. *(pleading)* You can't leave me alone with her.

GINA. I really should go.

TODDLE. Please. Be my secretary.

GINA. You don't want me, Mr. Toddle.

TODDLE. Of course I want you. You're perfect.

GINA. I'm not perfect.

TODDLE. What's wrong with you?

GINA. I have a wooden leg.

TODDLE. Oh God.

GINA. Yep.

> *(knuckle-rapping one of her legs)*

Knock on wood.

TODDLE. Is it the whole leg or do you just have a peg?

GINA. I can't be here anymore.

> *(She quickly exits, almost running into* **BEATRICE** *who is on her way in, carrying a glass of water.)*

BEATRICE. *(handing the glass to* **TODDLE**.*)* What's wrong? Your girlfriend seems upset.

TODDLE. *(absently)* We – uh – just broke up. It was destined to happen.

BEATRICE. You'll find someone else. Try on your new belt.

TODDLE. *(emotionally drained)* Oh yes. I should try on my new belt.

BEATRICE. *(mothering)* I won't be a stranger, Mr. Toddle. I'll be keeping an eye on you, don't you worry.

TODDLE. Yes. You do that, Mrs. Carpenter. You do that.

> *(Lights go out.)*

The Second Interview

DELORES CARR
TIMOTHINA RUSSELL

(Lights come up on **DELORES CARR** *who is busy arranging two chairs in front of her desk. A small tape recorder rests on the desk.* **DELORES** *sits down, glances at her watch, taps her foot. There is a KNOCK. She jumps up and goes out. A moment later she returns, escorting* **TIMOTHINA RUSSELL** *into her office.)*

DELORES. It's so nice to see you. You're my last interviewee.

TIMOTHINA. I *am?*

DELORES. *(gesturing for* **TIMOTHINA** *to sit.)* The very last. We should have champagne. This is a day for celebration.

*(*TIMOTHINA *sits.* DELORES *sits down as well.)*

TIMOTHINA. It *is?* How nice.

DELORES. I thought that the actual writing of the book would be the onerous part. But conducting all these interviews has been quite an undertaking. I think you're number one-hundred-fourteen.

TIMOTHINA. One-hundred-fourteen and the very last. Oh my. All of them face-to-face like this one?

DELORES. Maybe a third. The rest were phone interviews. I like this better. I like to look the person I'm interviewing straight in the eye.

TIMOTHINA. *(smiling)* It does help, doesn't it?

DELORES. Oh my God, yes. On the phone you can't tell if a person is pulling your leg. It's hard to gauge sincerity if you can't –

TIMOTHINA. Look a person straight in the eye. I quite agree.

DELORES. Shall we get down to business?

TIMOTHINA. I'm at your service.

DELORES. Now, there might be a tendency to agree with some of the things that the others have said, but I want you to go a step beyond simple corroboration if you would, and give me your honest, personal take on things. I really don't mind different perspectives. They provide shading and nuance.

(**TIMOTHINA** *nods.* **DELORES** *looks at her notes, switches on the tape recorder.*)

Now, you were personal assistant to Ms. Dowell for how many years? I want to get the dates right.

TIMOTHINA. A year-and-a-half. The first year and a half of President Dowell's first term.

DELORES. *(again, consulting her notes)* And I believe you left to take a job in New York – public relations or something, am I right?

TIMOTHINA. That's right. I went to work for a public relations firm in Manhattan.

DELORES. Now Quinnipiac recently did a survey – an attempt to rank, according to public opinion, the most popular First Ladies over the last one hundred years, and Lana Dowell placed at the very top. Higher than Eleanor Roosevelt. Higher than Hillary or Michelle. It was really quite remarkable, though understandable. When President Dowell left office, Ms. Dowell's approval rating, as I recall, was twenty points higher than that of her husband.

TIMOTHINA. Is that so? Well, people *were* sort of tired of the President.

DELORES. To what do *you* attribute her popularity?

TIMOTHINA. I wouldn't know.

DELORES. What do you mean?

TIMOTHINA. I mean I wouldn't know why she was so popular. For that matter, I don't know why she continues to get all the positive news coverage. She hasn't lived in the White House for over two years.

DELORES. People loved her. They still love her.

TIMOTHINA. They do, don't they?

DELORES. Let me see.

(consulting her notes)

Let's do this: describe the former First Lady for me in two or three words. Distill her down to her essence for me. At least the way *you* see her. Just who *is* Lana Dowell?

TIMOTHINA. *(pondering the challenge)* Two or three words.

DELORES. Yes. Give me two or three words that you feel best describe the former First Lady.

TIMOTHINA. All right.

(thinks for a moment, then:)

Spawn of Satan.

DELORES. Come again?

TIMOTHINA. Spawn of Satan.

(counting off with her fingers)

One, two, three words. Yes, that's how I would describe her.

*(**DELORES** stares at **TIMOTHINA** for a moment, not speaking. Then she breaks into a smile.)*

DELORES. You're being funny.

(beat)

Aren't you?

*(**TIMOTHINA** shakes her head.)*

Spawn of Satan. Come now.

TIMOTHINA. I'm sorry.

DELORES. No harm done.

TIMOTHINA. I should have said "a reeking pile of maggot-filled dung, shot out of Beelzebub's...derrière."

DELORES. *(switching off the tape recorder)* Ms. Russell, I don't know what to – If you weren't interested in doing this interview, you could have saved us both the time and trouble, and simply cancelled.

TIMOTHINA. But I didn't have anything better to do this afternoon and it really was a beautiful drive. Just like you said it would be.

DELORES. And yet what you just said –

TIMOTHINA. I was giving you my honest opinion.

DELORES. You can't possibly mean any of that.

TIMOTHINA. But I do. I think Lana Dowell is the worst human being I've met in my life, let alone had the sorry misfortune to have spent eighteen months working for.

DELORES. I'm really quite – I mean, Ms. Russell, if I may – I have just completed interviews with one-hundred-thirteen men and women who worked closely with the former First Lady – family members, people who to this day remain close friends with her. I interviewed her ninety-three-year-old Sunday school teacher, for crying out loud.

TIMOTHINA. *(matter-of-factly)* It sounds to me as if those people don't know her the way I do.

DELORES. Ms. Russell, do you have a personal vendetta against Ms. Dowell?

TIMOTHINA. No.

DELORES. I feel like I just climbed through the Looking Glass. Ms. Russell, you're wasting my time. I'm sorry I asked you here.

(She stands.)

TIMOTHINA. Is the interview over?

DELORES. It is.

*(**TIMOTHINA** rises.)*

TIMOTHINA. Suit yourself. Her husband was famous for not listening to dissenting voices and apparently his wife's biographer is just as uncomfortable with *my* minority opinion.

DELORES. Yours isn't a minority opinion, Ms. Russell. It's blatant character assassination, and it will not be recorded upon the pages of my biography.

TIMOTHINA. Suit yourself.

DELORES. Why do you keep saying that?

TIMOTHINA. Can you validate my parking stub?

(**DELORES** *stares at her. Her face says "no."*)

(*calmly and without rancor*) So, just to be clear: I drive quite some distance from my house. I spend three...

(*checks her watch*)

...possibly four dollars for the parking garage, only to be dismissed by you for simply telling you what the First Lady was *really* like.

DELORES. Ms. Russell, I have no idea what your problem with Ms. Dowell is, but one-hundred-thirteen –

TIMOTHINA. (*finishing her sentence*) ...people think she was a better First Lady than Eleanor Roosevelt, that she changed people's lives with a hug and a smile. I'm telling you that she has another side. But you don't want to hear it. You're writing the authorized biography and there's no place in an authorized biography for all the warts – or rather the festering sores upon that woman's character, which define her.

DELORES. Let someone else write that kind of book. It won't be me.

TIMOTHINA. I'd at least be curious, though. If I were you. I'd be more than a little curious.

DELORES. Why should I waste my time sitting here listening to you make these scandalous statements about a universally-admired public figure?

TIMOTHINA. Because I contend that she stopped being wonderful the day she pitched her sorority sister out of a two-story sorority-house window and put the girl in a neck brace for a year.

DELORES. And you're going to tell me that the girl was your sister. Or your cousin.

TIMOTHINA. I never met that poor stiff-necked woman in my life. It was Ms. Dowell herself who brought the incident to my attention.

DELORES. Ms. Dowell confessed to you that she pitched one of her sorority sisters out of an open second floor window?

TIMOTHINA. It wasn't open. There was substantial glass breakage.

(beat)

She was high on Angel Dust at the time.

DELORES. I won't even dignify this charge with a –

TIMOTHINA. *(interrupting)* One night. When she was in a confessional mood. She told me this and a whole lot more.

DELORES. There is no way on earth that I would ever believe you.

TIMOTHINA. You will when you hear it. Told in her own words. You see, I secretly recorded it.

DELORES. You didn't.

TIMOTHINA. I did. I have the whole drunken two-hour confession on tape. It's sitting in a safety deposit box at my bank.

DELORES. I cannot possibly –

TIMOTHINA. The animal abuse, the petty thefts, the incident in the church vestry.

DELORES. What incident in a – No, no, I refuse to hear it. I don't know what your game is, Ms. Russell, but I will not play it.

TIMOTHINA. Then publish your valentine to the First Lady, take your money and live with your conscience. At least I tried.

(She starts out.)

DELORES. Why haven't –

*(***TIMOTHINA*** *stops)*

Why haven't you come forward before now?

TIMOTHINA. *(turning)* Because I had no reason to before now. I felt it was better that no one should know about that side to her.

DELORES. So why – why today?

TIMOTHINA. Perhaps it was that poll. Or this interview. Perhaps it was the fact that she left office so unblemished, and it finally just got to me. It was always her husband who stumbled and her two sons who got the bad press, but Lana Dowell was the paragon of spousal and motherly virtue. Well, truth to tell, she wasn't. She had a dark side that she confessed to me the night before I left for New York. We drank too much wine and she got very relaxed. "You'll see that I've made a few mistakes," she said, "but nothing that ever got out. Because I've been very good at covering my tracks." She was quite proud of this fact. Well, here's a track that she didn't cover very well. And it's all on tape: the teenage rampage through that nursing home, the ex-lover she tried to run over with her Vespa, the night she smoked speedball with two child pornographers. It's all there. Even what happened in the church vestry.

DELORES. I don't want to hear what happened in the church vestry.

TIMOTHINA. Apparently you don't want to hear anything that happened anywhere.

DELORES. Even if what you're saying is true…

(**TIMOTHINA** *rebuts this with a scowl.*)

…there is no way I could put any of it in this book.

TIMOTHINA. Because it's an authorized puff bio.

DELORES. That, yes, and the fact that I'm being paid quite a bit of money to write it. Just five years ago I was on food stamps, Ms. Russell. I can't go back to that. This is my meal ticket. Literally.

TIMOTHINA. That's a dilemma. Of course there are publishers out there who would be willing to publish the *other* biography – the *un*authorized one. There would be publishers champing at the bit for that kind of exposé.

DELORES. But ethically – my God, Ms. Russell – think of all the lives she's saved with her private AIDS and Malaria initiatives. The woman has been personally responsible for lowering the country's illiteracy rate by at least fifteen percent.

TIMOTHINA. She defrocked a priest.

(beat)

While singing "Hava Nagila."

DELORES. When was this?

TIMOTHINA. She was twenty-something.

DELORES. *(after a long, thoughtful beat)* I believe that people can change. Do you not believe that? Do you not believe in redemption?

*(**TIMOTHINA** shrugs.)*

Let me ask you this: the last thing she allegedly confessed to you – how old was she? When was the last abominable act that she owned up to?

TIMOTHINA. I'm going to say twenty-two.

DELORES. Twenty-two. That would be – what? – thirty-five years ago.

TIMOTHINA. Or there about.

DELORES. And she's done nothing untoward since then.

TIMOTHINA. I believe that's right.

DELORES. But don't you see? Thirty-five years ago Lana Dowell –

TIMOTHINA. She wasn't Dowell back then. She was a Fitz-Binkle.

DELORES. Whatever. My point is that if she did commit all these atrocious acts when she was young, she went on to more than make up for it in her later years. In fact, she made up for it in such a big way that the whole world fell in love with her.

TIMOTHINA. Even the parents of those little girls she abandoned in Davy Crockett National Forest?

DELORES. What are you talking about?

TIMOTHINA. A certain Girl Scout outing that went so horribly, so terribly wrong.

DELORES. As the story was told to me, Lana was lost overnight *with* those little girls.

(**TIMOTHINA** *shakes her head.*)

What do you mean…

(**DELORES** *copies* **TIMOTHINA**'s *head-shake.*)

TIMOTHINA. Lana didn't spend the night with those girls. She spent it sniffing patio sealant with a couple of grizzled squirrel-hunters she met. She left those poor girls with only a broken cigarette lighter and two boxes of stale Samoas to get them through the night.

DELORES. I don't believe you.

TIMOTHINA. But let's say – for argument's sake – that everything I've told you is true. What would you do?

DELORES. Frankly, I don't know *what* I'd do.

TIMOTHINA. I'll tell you what you do: you don't write the book.

DELORES. By following your line of reasoning: does it really matter whether I write it or not? I mean, you're still going to be there waiting in the wings for the next biographer who comes along. Waiting there with your taped confession. I mean – if you actually *have* a taped confession.

(**TIMOTHINA** *grins cryptically.*)

What? *What?*

TIMOTHINA. If you decide not to write the book – *this* book – I just might be persuaded to destroy the tape.

DELORES. I don't understand.

TIMOTHINA. Do you think I really want all this to get out? I mean what do I get out of *that?*

DELORES. Then what is it you *do* want?

(**TIMOTHINA** *takes a moment to prepare herself; what she's about to say is important.*)

TIMOTHINA. A conscientious, principled ghost-writer to tell my own life story.

DELORES. To tell –

TIMOTHINA. The story of my own life. It's an incredible story. I've been looking for just the right person to put it all down for me. A person with integrity. Someone with scruples.

DELORES. You think I have scruples?

TIMOTHINA. I suspect that you do. You'll confirm my assumption if you give back your advance and tell your publisher that you're unable to finish that book.

DELORES. And what makes *your* story so special?

TIMOTHINA. *(relishing the unveiling of this revelation)* I was raised by monkeys.

DELORES. *(skeptical)* What?

(**TIMOTHINA** *illustrates this admission by scratching her armpits like a chimp.* **DELORES** *just stares.*)

TIMOTHINA. My father was an experimental anthropologist, you see. I lived with chimpanzees until I was seven. That's when I began hungering for a different kind of life. That's also about the time that Daddy was arrested for child endangerment.

DELORES. Uh huh.

TIMOTHINA. You think I'm kidding. It's all documented. Is your tape recorder on?

DELORES. This is ridiculous.

TIMOTHINA. You want to know. I see it in your face. Hear me out.

DELORES. I can't believe I'm –

TIMOTHINA. It's a very moving story.

DELORES. Chimpanzees.

TIMOTHINA. *(nodding)* And orangutans and one baboon. Oh, and a scruffy homeless boy named Roy whom Daddy brought home from the bus station one night.

(indicating the tape recorder)

Turn it on.

*(**DELORES** switches on the tape recorder.)*

My earliest memory…

(She leans in to get closer to the tape recorder.)

…was of being groomed by a hairy hand.

DELORES. I want to hear that tape.

TIMOTHINA. You'll hear it, you'll hear it. But first I want to tell you about Tamba and Zo-zo.

DELORES. *(surrendering, wearily)* Yes, you go right ahead and tell me all about Tamba and Zo-zo.

(Lights fade out.)

The Third Interview

FELICIA PENETTI
GORDON GREEN

(Lights come up on **FELICIA PENETTI** *and* **GORDON GREEN** *shaking hands.)*

FELICIA. I am so delighted you came. Won't you sit down?

(They both sit.)

I believe you told me on the phone that you're retired. Is that right?

GORDON. *(nodding)* For about two years now. I used to work for a company that sold above-ground swimming pools.

FELICIA. No health problems? Nothing like that?

GORDON. Oh no. The company was downsizing and I'd had enough of the swimming pool game. Thirty years is a long time for man to sell above-ground swimming pools in spite of all the wonderful advancements.

FELICIA. What do you do now – besides, of course, going out to the ballpark?

GORDON. My wife owns a little gift shop on the square. I help her out whenever she needs me. I've considered getting into real estate. I leave my options open.

FELICIA. Well, I'm glad you applied for the job as our team mascot. Are you fit, Mr. Green?

GORDON. How do you mean?

FELICIA. Are you in good shape? It's somewhat of a demanding job – I mean, physically.

GORDON. I'm no couch potato if that's what you want to know.

FELICIA. You're fifty-five.

GORDON. I golf, Ms. Penetti – by mare's shank.

FELICIA. Mare's shank?

GORDON. *(explaining, jocularly)* By me legs, Ms. Penetti. No golf cart. I also swim, and I try to get to the gym two, sometimes three times a week.

FELICIA. So I don't have to worry that all that jumping around at the ballpark might be injurious to your health.

GORDON. I can handle it.

FELICIA. Now, you're aware of course, that this job isn't for everyone. You're our...

(counting up in her head)

...fifth Simon.

GORDON. May I ask why the others quit? I mean, this is only the team's second season.

FELICIA. Various reasons. *Different* reasons.

GORDON. I mean, besides the obvious.

FELICIA. And what would you say is the "obvious" reason?

GORDON. The fact that your team's mascot is a centipede.

FELICIA. Well, the team *is* the 'Centipedes," Mr. Green. It only stands to reason that the mascot should be a centipede too.

GORDON. I've seen the costume. It's a little off-putting.

FELICIA. Yes it is. It *is* off-putting. Well hell, Mr. Green: it's downright frightening, that's what it is. But we're in the process of addressing that.

GORDON. What are you doing?

FELICIA. Well, we've removed a few of the legs. There aren't nearly as many as there were last season.

GORDON. And has that helped?

FELICIA. A little. I don't know. A couple of weeks ago we took Simon to an elementary school, you know, to gauge the reactions of the children after we'd removed some of the legs. But he didn't test as well as we would have liked.

GORDON. The kids still got scared?

FELICIA. Yes. Well, not all of them.

(beat)

FELICIA. *(cont.)* There were a couple of blind children there. They said he was soft.

GORDON. I've never understood why the mascot has to be a centipede. Couldn't you think of something a little more child-friendly?

FELICIA. Well, we wanted to. The general manager pleaded with the owner for permission to go in a different direction. We had our costume designer come up with some nice, very generic baseball-ish mascot concepts. Betty the Baseball Bat. Homey Home Plate. Captain Capp – you know, a baseball cap with arms and legs. Mr. Van Willingham shot them all down.

GORDON. Captain Capp doesn't sound like a bad idea.

FELICIA. I like it too, but Mr. Van Willingham hates it. He said there is nothing more ridiculous than a cap moving through the stands not affixed to a person's head.

GORDON. But what does he say when you bring back these reports about Simon Centipede – about how he's scaring all the kids?

FELICIA. And a few of the adults too. Van Willingham doesn't bat an eye. Why should he? It's still free advertising for his Arachno-rarium.

GORDON. *(nodding)* I'd almost forgotten that Van Willingham owns the Arachno-rarium. Yes, I can see the connection.

FELICIA. It's why he named the team the Centipedes.

GORDON. There isn't another arachnid he could have named the team after?

FELICIA. There are plenty. What would *you* go with? Spiders? Scorpions? Ticks? Daddy-long legs?

GORDON. People like Daddy-long legs.

FELICIA. But you see – they're all *legs*, Mr. Green. Hardly any body to them at all. I don't even see how they can survive with such a tiny body. And how in the world are you going to create a mascot costume that's all legs and no body?

GORDON. *(suddenly seized by a thought)* Wait a minute. A centipede isn't an arachnid. It's a chilipod.

FELICIA. A what?

GORDON. A chilipod. A centipede isn't an arachnid at all.

FELICIA. Are you sure about this?

GORDON. I'm almost positive. My kid was really into the creepy crawlies.

FELICIA. Let me check.

(She opens up her laptop and taps on it. She looks at the screen.)

GORDON. What are you doing?

FELICIA. I'm googling "centipede." Now I'm going to Wikipedia.

GORDON. *(weak attempt at humor)* Because there isn't a "Centipedia"?

FELICIA. *(all business)* Yes. Clever. Now here we are. Class: Chilipoda. Not Class: Arach – what would it be?

GORDON. Arachnida. Or something like that.

FELICIA. I'll be damned.

GORDON. See?

FELICIA. I'm stunned.

GORDON. You would think –

FELICIA. Yes you *would* think. You would think that a man who builds a zoo for arachnids would have a better idea of what is an arachnid and what isn't an arachnid. He's got centipedes...

GORDON. And millipedes.

FELICIA. ...slithering all over that zoo.

(She picks up the phone.)

I can't believe we went along with all this nonsense for so long.

GORDON. Who are you calling?

FELICIA. Mr. Tyrone, the general manager. Frightening little children. You should have seen the faces of those poor first graders when Simon the Centipede walked in on all those legs – it was enough to break your –

(She's interrupted by a voice on the other end.)

Julie. This is Felicia. Hi. Is Mr. Tyrone in?

(listens, then into phone)

He is?

(covering phone, to **GORDON***)*

Speak of the devil! Mr. Tyrone's got Mr. Van W –

(into phone)

Julie – on second thought, I wonder if I could speak with Mr. Van Willingham.

*(***FELICIA*** listens.)*

(still into phone) Well, this is important too. It's quite important.

(listens, then into phone)

Thank you.

(to **GORDON***)*

She's going to ask Mr. Van Willingham if he'll speak with me.

GORDON. What are you going to do?

FELICIA. Well, I'm going to tell the old coot that –

(into phone)

Hello, Mr. Van Willingham. I'm sorry to interrupt your meeting. Mr. Van Willingham, are you aware that a centipede isn't an arachnid?

(listens)

Because I'm looking at an article about them.

(reacting squeamishly to what she sees on the screen)

One of them is staring right at me with his –

(turning to **GORDON***)*

With his what?

GORDON. His eyes?

(quickly corrects himself.)

No, no. His *ocelli.*

FELICIA. *(into phone)* The class is Chilopoda, Mr. Van Willingham. Not Arachnida.

(listens)

Well, they're *all* arthropods, sir. It's a big phylum. Centipedes, tarantulas, insects – all sorts of insects. Crabs. Lobsters. Some arthopods are even edible it appears.

(listens)

I'm telling you this, sir, because as much as I respect your business acumen, you've confused arthropods with arachnids. It's a deadly mistake. I think that mistake came from your eagerness to open your spider and centipede zoo and give everyone the squeals. But, Mr. Van Willingham, you're not getting squeals at the ballpark. You're getting children hiding under the seats and you're getting revulsion from the parents. Your park attendance numbers are plummeting and here's your reason, and you know what, Mr. Van Willingham? It doesn't even have to be this way.

(listens)

Uh huh. Uh huh.

(listens)

Are you sure you want to do that?

(listens)

Well, if that's what you want to do. Do you want me to wait?

(listens)

All right.

GORDON. What's he doing?

FELICIA. *(to* GORDON*)* He's firing his general manager. I'm to be the new general manager of the Johnson City Lobsters.

(into phone) Yes sir. I'll be right over.

(She returns the phone receiver to its cradle and stares at it in amazement.)

GORDON. Um. *Congratulations?*

FELICIA. *(all smiles)*

Yes. Yes indeed. Thank you, Mr. Green.

(She gets up and steps away from her desk during the following. GORDON *also rises.)*

He's going to fire everyone at his Arachno-rarium. He's going to close it down and reopen it as an Arthropodarium. There's going to be a high-end seafood restaurant. I'm sure he'll make a bundle.

GORDON. He really didn't know?

FELICIA. I think he did. I think he was waiting for someone to correct him. A whole year – not a single person told the man he was wrong.

GORDON. I guess they were all afraid of losing their jobs. There's an irony for you.

FELICIA. To be honest with you, Mr. Green, I don't know why *I* did it. Yes I do. You gave me the courage.

GORDON. I did?

(She nods.)

Thank you then, I guess.

FELICIA. I have to go. Mr. Van Willingham is waiting for me.

GORDON. Yes, of course.

FELICIA. I appreciate everything you've done for me.

GORDON. *(bashful)* It was nothing.

(beat)

So what about the, *um,* job?

FELICIA. Oh, the *job*! Yes! It appears, Mr. Green, that you're going to be a lobster now.

GORDON. *(smiling and nodding)* I think I'd like to be a lobster. Chelae are funny.

FELICIA. What?

GORDON. Chelae. The, uh, *claws*. The kids'll get a kick out of my big mitts.

FELICIA. I'll walk you out.

(They start out of the room.)

I hated that damned centipede. He used to give me the willies. And I'm not even six years old.

GORDON. I'm sorry to hear that.

FELICIA. I feel like a new woman.

GORDON. That's great. And *I'm* going to be a lobster.

FELICIA. This was tidy.

GORDON. Couldn't be tidier.

(They walk out as lights fade out.)

The Fourth Interview

DR. JUDY GABLE
FRANK HALLOWELL
YVONNE SIMS

(Lights come up on **DR. JUDY GABLE** *writing at her desk. Her phone intercom buzzes.)*

INTERCOM VOICE (FEMALE). Your three-thirty is here, Doctor.

JUDY. Thank you, Kelli. Will you send him in?

(A moment later **FRANK HALLOWELL** *enters. The two shake hands.)*

FRANK. Sorry. I'm a little late.

JUDY. Hardly at all. Have a seat.

(They sit down.)

I should have warned you: on Friday afternoons downtown traffic gets pretty snarly around four – everybody trying to get a jump on the weekend. You said over the phone that you've never been to a psychologist before.

FRANK. That's right. *Or* to a psychiatrist.

JUDY. There's a "doctor" in front of my name, but I'm a psychologist. And feel free to call me Judy.

FRANK. All right.

JUDY. Now, let's find out if I can help you. If I think I can help you, we'll talk about setting up a weekly appointment for you.

FRANK. How will you know?

JUDY. Know what?

FRANK. If you can help me.

JUDY. Well, that's what this preliminary interview will determine.

FRANK. Oh.

JUDY. Are we on the same page?

FRANK. *(without enthusiasm)* Yes, of course.

JUDY. Mr. Hallowell, may I say something?

FRANK. Sure.

JUDY. You don't sound very *invested* in this.

FRANK. To be honest, Dr. –

> *(quickly correcting himself)*

> *Judy.* Coming here wasn't my idea. It was my wife's.

JUDY. That's not so unusual. And please don't call me Dr. Judy. Just Judy is fine. So tell me, Frank: why does your wife think you need to see a psychologist?

FRANK. Well, she's decided that I'm losing my marbles.

JUDY. Is that how she put it?

FRANK. No. That's how *I* put it. She just says I'm nuts.

JUDY. Based on…?

FRANK. Based on the way I've been acting. The things I've been saying.

JUDY. And how have you been acting, Frank? What is it you've been saying?

FRANK. *(after taking a couple of breaths to put himself into the moment)* "Stop it! Turn it off! Turn off the damned music!"

JUDY. Music?

FRANK. Yes.

JUDY. Who's playing music?

FRANK. I don't know.

JUDY. You're hearing music and you don't know where it's coming from?

FRANK. That's right.

JUDY. You literally *do not* know where it's coming from?

FRANK. That's what I said.

JUDY. But you *do* know, don't you?

FRANK. Huh?

JUDY. It's in your head, isn't it? The music. That's where it is: in your head.

FRANK. *(matter-of-factly)* No. It isn't in my head.

JUDY. A tune that haunts you night and day.

FRANK. What?

JUDY. "A pretty girl is like a melody that haunts you night and day." It's *that* kind of music, isn't it?

FRANK. No it isn't.

JUDY. Then where is the music, Frank?

FRANK. I honestly don't know. Out *there*. Somewhere out there. It follows me around. I can't get away from it.

JUDY. And there's no chance that it's simply ambient music you're hearing: a neighbor's stereo? A car radio? It isn't the college marching band practicing for Saturday's game?

FRANK. No, Judy, I think I could identify music being played by a college marching band. It isn't like any of those things you just said.

JUDY. Then what does it sound like? Tell me.

FRANK. I've thought about this a lot.

JUDY. Yes?

FRANK. And here's the best way I know how to put it: it sounds like I'm in the middle of my own movie. It sounds like a – uh – what's the word?

JUDY. A soundtrack?

FRANK. Right. A movie soundtrack. *Underscoring*. That's it. It sounds like my life – like every day of my life is being underscored.

JUDY. What about right now, Frank? Do you hear the music right now? While we're sitting here talking?

FRANK. No.

JUDY. No music. None.

FRANK. Sometimes it stops. It's like a movie that way too. Sometimes there's music. Sometimes there isn't.

JUDY. And are there certain times you'd be more likely to hear the music?

FRANK. Well, I made a chart. I don't know if it will be much help to you, though.

(He takes out a folded piece of paper from his pocket and opens it up. He hands it to **JUDY**.*)*

As you can see, there's really no logic to it. No predicting when I'm going to hear it.

JUDY. *(looking over the chart)* It's quite haphazard, isn't it?

FRANK. *(nodding)* I was looking for some sort of pattern. There doesn't seem to be one. As you can see.

(pointing to a spot on the piece of paper)

This morning, for example. I heard music while I was shaving and brushing my teeth. Then silence during breakfast. Then music again in the car driving to work. I work at an insurance company. This was a particularly long stretch. It didn't stop until lunch. It's been quiet since then.

JUDY. What kind of music is it, Frank?

FRANK. What do you mean?

JUDY. Is it Jazz? Classical? Is it Rockabilly music, Frank?

FRANK. *(thinking)* Well, I don't –

JUDY. Does it distract you? Is it dissonant? Is it nice? I mean, would you like it under other circumstances? Does it calm you or does it make you edgy? Are there voices that sing along with the music?

FRANK. No voices. It's all instrumental. And it isn't all that bad. I mean it's really very pretty sometimes. Very interesting, you know, harmonically or whatever you call it. But that's one of the problems: I sometimes find myself not getting anything done. I just sit there listening to it.

JUDY. Enjoying it?

FRANK. Sometimes. But usually it's very inconvenient. And sometimes it's too loud. I can't hear the television. I'm blasting the volume on the TV and Dana –

JUDY. Dana?

FRANK. That's my wife. She has to sit there like we're a couple of old fogies in the nursing home with the sound on the TV turned all the way up. Lately, she's been getting up and going into the bedroom. And I think she's crying in there, but, of course, I can't hear her over the music, so I'm not sure.

JUDY. That's why she wanted you to come see me.

FRANK. Dana – see, she thinks it's all in my head. Just like you did. She doesn't understand. But I can't explain it to her. I agreed to come here – to do this thing for her. She thinks I'm doing this for our marriage.

JUDY. You're not?

FRANK. There's something else that I...

JUDY. Yes?

FRANK. ...that I need to tell you.

JUDY. All right.

FRANK. I'm not the only one who hears it.

JUDY. Someone else hears the music.

FRANK. That's right.

JUDY. And who is this person? This someone else.

FRANK. I met her about a week ago. At Arby's. Her name is Yvonne. I was sitting in the booth next to hers. And the music started playing. And I could tell by the look on her face that she could hear it too.

JUDY. You could tell this by the expression on her face?

FRANK. *(nodding)* And by the fact that she was kind of tick-tocking her head back and forth like a metronome.

(He demonstrates.)

JUDY. So you...

FRANK. Asked her. Point blank.

JUDY. *And...*

FRANK. She confirmed it.

JUDY. I see.

FRANK. And she asked if I wanted to join her. And it was the strangest thing. We just sat there like *this*...

(His head becomes metronomic again.)

...and then the music got a little bouncier, and little more, you know, *peppier.*

JUDY. "Peppier?"

(FRANK is swaying now, relating physically to the music as he's remembering it.)

FRANK. And I knew this was going to happen, because this was a song I'd heard before. So *I'm* grooving...

JUDY. *(over FRANK)* "Grooving"?

FRANK. ...and *she's* grooving –

JUDY. *(interrupting)* Some of the music repeats itself?

FRANK. Most music is unavoidably derivative, don't you think?

JUDY. I wouldn't know.

FRANK. Anyway, in no time at all we're both humming right along, as natural as can be. Just like we'd been doing this all of our lives. And in her case that's almost true.

(beat, smiling)

It was the happiest moment of my life.

JUDY. And why is that, Frank? Why was this the happiest moment of your life?

FRANK. Because of what it told me. It told me that I wasn't going insane, after all. I almost cancelled this appointment.

JUDY. But you didn't.

FRANK. No, I promised Dana I'd come. So I came.

JUDY. I don't know what to say.

FRANK. Maybe you don't know what to say because there isn't anything wrong with me. Apparently there is this music out there. And most people can't hear it. But a few people can. And for good or bad I'm one of those people. And so is Yvonne.

JUDY. So you think there are other people – I mean even besides you and Yvonne – who can hear the music?

FRANK. I do. And we've decided to go looking for them.

JUDY. And the "why" doesn't matter.

FRANK. What do you mean?

JUDY. I mean that it doesn't matter *why* you and Yvonne are hearing this music that most people aren't hearing and which you've decided doesn't represent a form of mental illness.

FRANK. No. I'm just saying there's a chance we'll never know for sure what's going on here. But we don't plan to waste the rest our lives trying to figure it out. We're just going to let ourselves feel good about the fact that we aren't alone. What's wrong with that?

JUDY. There's nothing at all wrong with that. I do think, though, that I'm going to need some time to process this.

FRANK. Then just go right ahead and process it. In the mean time how about you and me – we tell Dana that there really wasn't any need for me to come here today? Why don't we do *that*, Judy?

JUDY. I'm not sure I want to do that. At least not yet.

FRANK. Why?

JUDY. You said the music can be distracting. You said that your wife goes into the bedroom some nights and cries.

FRANK. That isn't an issue anymore.

JUDY. And why is that?

FRANK. Because I'm going to ask her for a divorce. I want to marry Yvonne.

JUDY. Things are moving awfully fast, don't you think?

FRANK. I think people need to be with those who understand what they're going through. You can't deny that Yvonne understands what I'm going through.

JUDY. Then maybe I'm *not* the best person to help you.

FRANK. And maybe I don't even need help. Maybe I just need to learn how to live with my disability. Yvonne's been hearing the music since she was a little girl. She's learned how to deal with it. She'll help *me* to deal with it. She's outside, by the way. Do you want to meet her?

JUDY. She's here?

FRANK. *(nodding)* She had to buy a pack of gum. She's probably back now. She's probably sitting right outside in your waiting room.

JUDY. *(into intercom)* Kelli, is there someone out there with you? A friend of Mr. Hallowell's?

INTERCOM VOICE. She's right here. Do you want me to send her in?

JUDY. *(after a moment's consideration)* Yes. Why don't you do that?

(A moment later **YVONNE SIMS** *enters. Both* **JUDY** *and* **FRANK** *get up.* **YVONNE** *and* **JUDY** *shake hands.)*

JUDY. Hello, Yvonne. Frank's been telling me a little about you.

YVONNE. *(to* **FRANK***)* You didn't tell her about the time I got kicked out of Symphony Hall, did you?

(to **JUDY***)*

They were playing Beethoven's *Eroica* but I was getting this crazy Charles Ives-like total polytonal mishmash coming into both my ears and I just lost it.

JUDY. You lost it?

YVONNE. Went all squirrelly. You know: too many notes.

FRANK. Yvonne knows music. She knows when it's too many notes.

YVONNE. *(mock confidential)* I've learned the language of my tormenters.

JUDY. This *is* fascinating.

YVONNE. See, Frankie. I told you there was a chance she'd believe you.

(to **JUDY***)*

I have the names of several people I found on the Internet who say they're going through the same thing.

If they're for real I'm going to ask if they'd like to join our affinitygroup.

JUDY. *(indulgent)* That's good. That's a step in the right direction.

(We now hear a car alarm going off nearby.)

Damn!

(She goes to an implied window, turns her back to the audience to look out.)

That blasted car alarm's been going off every other hour or so.

YVONNE. You sure it isn't a house alarm?

JUDY. No, I'm pretty sure it's a —

YVONNE. Like somebody just breaking into the same house over and over again, because, like, they're having trouble locating the family silver?

JUDY. You have quite an imagination.

YVONNE. Oh, I see where this is going.

JUDY. Where do you think this is going?

YVONNE. Why don't you just say it now and save us the time?

JUDY. Say what?

YVONNE. That it's my imagination that's responsible for all this music I hear. See, Frankie, I told you there was a good chance she wouldn't believe us. Come on, let's blow.

*(**FRANK** and **JUDY** start out. Suddenly the pulse of the car alarm becomes intricately rhythmic. The two stop and listen. After a moment, the rhythmic pattern changes. The alarm stops being an alarm. It takes on a softer, less blaring form of instrumentation. What we're hearing still isn't music — not quite yet — but it's getting close, and it's very interesting and quite listenable.)*

YVONNE. *(listening intently)* Oh that's wild. I like that.

FRANK. *(also listening intently)* Oh yeah. Oh, *yeah.*

*(Now **JUDY**, who has been positioned so that we've been unable to see her initial reaction to what **YVONNE** and **FRANK** have been hearing, turns around. Her face registers pure terror.)*

YVONNE. *(reacting to the look)* Oh my God!

FRANK. *(to **YVONNE**)* Do you think…?

YVONNE. She hears it! Look at her! Our affinity group is about to get its third member.

JUDY. What are you talking about?

YVONNE. *(to **JUDY**)* That base line. You *do* hear it, right?

JUDY. *(in denial)* It's a car alarm.

YVONNE. *(shaking her head)* It's more than that and you know it.

*(to **FRANK**)*

She's fighting it.

*(to **JUDY**)*

Don't fight it, Judy. Let it envelope you. Become one with the music.

(A beautiful melody now layers itself over the rhythmic base line. Clearly defined music is now invading the room.)

FRANK. She knows what's happening. Don't you, Judy? You know what's going on here, don't you?

JUDY. I – I – I –

YVONNE. *(enraptured)* Oh the *magic*! Oh the *mystery*!

FRANK. Really cool, huh?

JUDY. This can't possibly be.

YVONNE. And yet it *is*, Judy. It *is*!

*(**JUDY** goes to the intercom.)*

JUDY. Kelli?

INTERCOM VOICE. Yes?

JUDY. Do you hear that music?

INTERCOM VOICE. What music?

JUDY. It's very loud.

INTERCOM VOICE. What's very loud?

JUDY. You don't hear it?

INTERCOM VOICE. I don't hear anything, Dr. Gable. Am I supposed to be hearing something?

JUDY. *(still into intercom)* Go home, Kelli. Go on home.

(**JUDY** *stares at* **FRANK** *and* **YVONNE** *without speaking as the music continues to play, though it will, from this point on, begin a very slow fade-out.*)

I'm frightened.

YVONNE. Perfectly understandable. It was scary for me the first time too. I wet myself. I was eight.

FRANK. I wet *my*self. I was *forty*-eight.

JUDY. Will it ever go away?

YVONNE. It comes and goes. But it never stays away for long. I have a theory that everyone will be hearing it some day. That Frank and me – *and* you: we are the vanguard.

JUDY. I don't want to be part of a vanguard.

FRANK. I don't think you have much of a choice. You don't want to walk around with your ears all plugged up, do you?

YVONNE. Or your auditory nerves severed. That would be baby with the bathwater, wouldn't it, Frank?

FRANK. Baby with the bathwater. You got it, baby.

JUDY. Why is it happening?

FRANK. Again with the why.

(*to* **YVONNE**)

Always gotta know the why.

JUDY. But I *need* to know. I'm a scientist – of sorts. I have to know things. Who writes it? Who writes the music?

FRANK. *(philosophical)* Why are we here?

JUDY. Who plays it? Who decides when it will play and when it won't?

FRANK. When did time begin?

JUDY. Why do certain people hear it and others don't?

FRANK. Why are the mentally-challenged invariably given bad hair-cuts?

JUDY. Why are you making light of all this?

YVONNE. It's a coping mechanism, Dr. Gable. I have been teaching Frank how to cope. It is what gets me through each day. I cope. I deal. Sometimes I even *prefer* the music – can't imagine my life without it now. My aunt had a wind chime, Dr. Gable. And I used to sit out on her porch and listen as the breeze blew through that chime and I never knew what notes I was going to hear – what kind of little song that chime would sing to me. And it was a strange thing: hearing music that created itself, but over the years that wind chime stopped teasing me and I came to accept it. I couldn't see the agent behind it – the wind has no face, you know – but I embraced it as something only half-knowable. Now this music, Dr. Gable, it, too, is only half-knowable. It's knowable in the sense that we hear it and it caresses our ears – or *assaults* them depending on how it's being received. But it's also *un*knowable in the sense of not knowing where the hell it comes from. Now, I ask you this, Dr. Gable...

FRANK. Judy. She prefers to be called Judy.

YVONNE. Judy. I ask you this: do you want to spend the rest of your life driving yourself insane trying to solve the mystery of the music? Or do you simply want to enjoy it when it's pleasant and learn how to tolerate it when it isn't?

JUDY. Probably the latter. Yes, it would probably be best for me to do the latter.

YVONNE. Then you're just as sane as we are.

JUDY. I can't believe this is happening to me.

FRANK. You'll get used to it in time. I don't rail against it nearly as much as I used to.

JUDY. It broke up your marriage.

FRANK. No it didn't. Dana was having an affair with her tennis instructor. But that's neither here nor there.

(The music has ended.)

JUDY. *(attending the silence)* It stopped.

YVONNE. Sometimes it makes only a brief appearance. But it won't be a stranger.

FRANK. *(from "A Pretty Girl Is Like a Melody")* "Just like the strain of a haunting refrain."

JUDY. I don't know if I can do this.

YVONNE. What are your options, honey?

(JUDY sits down. She is numb. FRANK gives a look of concern.)

(to FRANK) She'll be okay. She's going to be fine. We're the special ones. Aren't we the special ones, Frank?

(FRANK sits down, nodding silently. YVONNE goes and stands next to him, taking his hand. HE reaches out with his other hand and takes JUDY's.)

YVONNE. It's okay. Everything's okay.

JUDY. It's so quiet now.

YVONNE. Some days – the silence...

FRANK. Pure bliss.

YVONNE. Shhh. Let's enjoy it while it lasts.

(The three don't move, as lights slowly fade out, JUDY shedding silent tears.)

The Fifth Interview

MYRA HENDERSON

DEANNE SPRAWLEY

HUCK GLEASON

*(Lights come up on **MYRA HENDERSON**, sitting at her desk. We hear a knock.)*

MYRA. Yes? Come in.

*(**DEANNE SPRAWLEY** and **HUCK GLEASON** enter. He is dressed in overalls. **MYRA** gets up from her desk and goes to greet the two with handshakes.)*

DEANNE. We're a little early. I hope that was all right.

MYRA. Perfectly fine. I might even get home a little earlier than usual tonight. Please sit down.

*(All sit down. **MYRA** looks at **HUCK** for a moment as if trying to figure out who he is.)*

DEANNE. I'm sorry. I'm so spacey these days. This is my father.

HUCK. Gleason. Huck Gleason.

(indicating his clothing)

Sorry about the − I was over at the seed and feed here in town. 'Didn't have time to go all the way home and change.

DEANNE. I drafted my father at the last minute. To come with me. I hope that's all right.

MYRA. Quite all right.

*(to **DEANNE**)*

You and Tommy live with Mr. Gleason now?

DEANNE. That's right. We moved in with Daddy a few weeks after my husband died.

MYRA. I knew you'd put the house on the market. I didn't know you weren't still living there.

DEANNE. I'm sorry. I didn't think to give you an address change. Tom and I always used a post office box for our mail anyway.

MYRA. It's important to keep our records up to date, but I understand, given the circumstances, why it may have slipped your mind.

HUCK. *(digging into his pocket)* I got –

DEANNE. Daddy's got the tuition check for the new semester. Something else that slipped my mind.

MYRA. So Tommy wants to stay on with us.

DEANNE. Yes. And Daddy's going to help out with the tuition.

(HUCK continues to look from pocket to pocket for the check.)

DEANNE. *(cont., to HUCK)* Do you have it? Maybe *I* have it.

(She opens up her shoulder bag. Together she and HUCK search for the check while MYRA looks on uncomfortably.)

MYRA. *(after another moment)* Why don't we just – Let's just talk about Tommy for right now.

(DEANNE and HUCK suspend their search.)

DEANNE. I know his grades have slipped. I knew this even before I got the report card.

MYRA. That's perfectly understandable after what he's been through.

DEANNE. He was in the car with his father when it overturned.

MYRA. Yes, I know.

DEANNE. You can imagine how he must feel.

HUCK. My son-in-law was thrown through the windshield. But now, Tommy, see – he had on the seatbelt. Seatbelt saved his life.

(feels something through the fabric of his overalls.)

Here it is. Got it right chere.

(He pulls out the check and hands it to **MYRA**. *She holds it for a moment, looks at it, then gives it back to* **HUCK**.*)*

MYRA. I'm sorry. We can't –

DEANNE. What's wrong?

HUCK. *(looking at the check)* I didn't put the right amount on it?

MYRA. No, that isn't the issue. The board has decided that it wouldn't be wise for Tommy to stay on with us.

DEANNE. But wait. I know we can pull his grades up. Tommy's a very smart little boy. He just needs some time to get over what's happened. That's what the doctor said. He said it takes a while for a child to recover from something like this.

MYRA. Yes. I understand. And his teachers – they've – well, we've *all* been very patient with him.

DEANNE. Then why are you kicking him out of your school?

*(*MYRA *takes a deep breath. It is obvious that she's been preparing for this moment for some time.)*

MYRA. Ms. Sprawley – this is a Christian school.

DEANNE. Yes, I know that. That's why I send Tommy here.

MYRA. And as such, Evangelical Christian Academy has a reputation to uphold – a reputation which is closely aligned with the mission of the school. Now you must know the mission of this school, Ms. Sprawley.

DEANNE. I believe I do.

MYRA. *(as* **DEANNE** *half-mouths the words of the mission statement along with her)* "To educate and inspire the whole person for the glory of God. To teach each child to become a faithful disciple of our Lord Jesus Christ." We're here to train and nurture our young people to spiritual maturity in Christ Jesus, Ms. Sprawley.

DEANNE. Yes, I know all of this. Why are you telling me this?

MYRA. If a child is disruptive – if a child makes it difficult for us to maintain the sort of atmosphere that best serves that mission, that best serves the spiritual needs of the students – simply put, Ms. Sprawley, it is required that the child be removed from the school.

DEANNE. That's what's happening right now? You're telling me that Tommy is being expelled?

MYRA. Well, I wouldn't –

DEANNE. You're kicking him out.

MYRA. We're asking that he not come back.

DEANNE. What has he done? What has my son done besides spending maybe a little too much time in the little boy's room crying over his dead father?

MYRA. It isn't *that,* Ms. Sprawley. We've certainly tolerated –

(quickly correcting herself)

We have been quite attentive to Tommy's special needs through this most difficult time.

DEANNE. So there's something else?

MYRA. Tommy hasn't said anything to you over the last couple of weeks? About school? About what's been going on here?

DEANNE. To be honest with you, Ms. Henderson, Tommy doesn't have much to say to me about *anything* these days. He spends most of his time up in his room, except when Daddy asks him to help a little with the chores. And I don't let him take his meals up there.

MYRA. I see.

DEANNE. If he's been acting out, Ms. Henderson, this is the first I've heard about it. Why hasn't his teacher called me?

MYRA. Ms. Grayson has asked that I handle this.

DEANNE. I just think it's – well, it's just incredibly unfair to make Tommy leave the school when you and I and Ms. Grayson – we haven't had even a single conversation about what's wrong. I thought there were supposed to be parent-teacher conferences when things get a little out of hand.

MYRA. *This* is the conference.

DEANNE. This isn't a conference. This is you telling me that Tommy doesn't get to go to Evangelical Christian any more. He has friends here. I mean, he *used* to, before –

(She stops herself.)

MYRA. Ms. Sprawley, I've tried to set up two meetings with you, if you will recall. Last week, the week before that. You called to cancel both of them. I'm almost surprised to see you here tonight.

DEANNE. My work schedule changed at my second job. I've had to put in more hours since Tom died. I'm sorry I blew you off, I really am. My life is one big mess right now, as you can imagine.

MYRA. I'm sorry to hear that, Ms. Sprawley, but the fact of the matter is that this is a problem that isn't going to be easily fixed. And rather than let this thing fester or get out of control, the board decided that it was probably best for your son to go to another school. Or have you considered home schooling?

DEANNE. *(an angry outburst)* How in God's name would I find time to do *that?*

HUCK. It's okay, pumpkin. Calm yourself, girl.

DEANNE. *(to MYRA)* This is how you handle your discipline problems? You just shove the kid out the front door of the school?

MYRA. This is more than a simple discipline problem.

DEANNE. What's he doing? What is my child doing? I'll take him to a counselor. I'll get a third job if I have to, to pay for it. Tommy loves this school. He would be crushed if he had to leave.

HUCK. You don't got to get another job, Dee. *I'll* pay for the counselor.

MYRA. *(slightly overlapping with HUCK)* He doesn't love the school, Ms. Sprawley.

DEANNE. What?

MYRA. I said that it is apparent to me and to the board that your son doesn't love this school at all. He'd rather be somewhere else. If you asked him, he'd tell you.

DEANNE. *(an outburst)* For the love of God, Ms. Henderson, *what is he doing?*

MYRA. *(with some difficulty)* He takes the name of God in vain. Repeatedly.

(beat)

He curses God. In front of the other children.

DEANNE. I don't – how do you mean?

MYRA. Exactly that. Just a couple of days ago he disrupted Bible class by sitting in the back of the room and – well, I'm not even going to say it.

DEANNE. Ms. Henderson, if you're going to eject my son from this school for something he's been saying, then I have every right to know what it was.

MYRA. He sat at the back of the room, if you must know, and said, "Damn God. Damn Jesus." Other times he tells his classmates that there *isn't* a God. He says Jesus is like Santa Claus and the Easter Bunny.

HUCK. Some people believe that, Ms. Henderson – cain't deny there's a bunch of non-believers out there.

MYRA. But you can understand why we'd prefer not to have them attending our school.

DEANNE. *(to MYRA)* You know he doesn't believe it. He's angry, that's all. He's mad at everybody because his daddy had to go away. Can you not understand it for what it is?

MYRA. I don't know whether he believes it or not. I only know that he is a negative influence on the other children.

DEANNE. Because he's dealing badly with the death of his father? This doesn't make any sense. What happened to Christian charity?

MYRA. We have been nothing *but* charitable to Tommy since your husband died. But it doesn't do any good. He talks during the prayers.

DEANNE. What does he say?

MYRA. The same sort of thing. Do we really have to – He blames God for the death of his father. That is, those days in which he decides that there *is* a God. Most days he says God doesn't exist.

DEANNE. But the very fact that he can't make up his mind about whether there's a God or not should be proof that –

MYRA. But on those days when he's decided that there *is* a God – well, then, it's all *God's* fault that his father died. It wasn't the rain-slick road. It wasn't the possibility that Mr. Sprawley had been driving too fast around that curve, given the hazardous conditions.

HUCK. My son-in-law was a good driver. Tommy said he was swerving to miss a deer.

MYRA. You're missing my point. It wasn't God's fault. Let's say that it was nobody's fault. Tommy nonetheless puts doubt in the other children's heads. Some of them have come to me – after having listened to him – have come to me confused, asking all sorts of questions.

DEANNE. So a person should never question?

MYRA. A person with a strong faith doesn't have to question. We raise these children in such a way as to strengthen and cement their faith, not knock it down. Tommy once said that his father was an atheist.

DEANNE. That's right. It was a major concession to Daddy and me that Tom allowed him to go to this school.

(laughs to herself)

That's an irony. Tom would get such a laugh out of *this*.

MYRA. I think that your husband may have been a negative influence on the boy – may have told him things that, with your husband's death, have only served to exacerbate this situation.

DEANNE. You've thought this all out. You and the board. To justify what you're doing. You've decided that Tommy has had the seeds of doubt planted in him. Kick him out now before things get *really* out of hand – before Tommy gets to high school and becomes a full-fledged subversive.

MYRA. The way you talk, Ms. Sprawley, I don't know why you would even *want* your son going to a school like this. Do you yourself – do *you* still believe in what Evangelical Christian stands for?

DEANNE. I used to. I used to believe in a lot of things. I have lost my husband, Ms. Henderson. My own faith has been severely tested. Perhaps I've lost that too. Tommy and I – with my father's help – we're just trying to get through each day as it comes. It really sucks, Ms. Henderson. Life sucks. God isn't smiling on Tommy and me right now. I don't blame Tommy for anything he says or does. If he's hurting another child, that's another matter. But questioning the existence of God when circumstances don't give you much of a reason to believe – I don't think that's such an odd thing to be doing. It tells me that Tommy is working his way through this the best he can. And I understand the anger. And I understand the betrayal because I feel it too. But what I *don't* understand is people like *you*, Ms. Henderson. Controlling kinds of people. That's what this school is – I've come to see it now. You control little minds. You put little minds in very tight boxes and punish those who don't stay put. Faith to me has always been a journey of discovery – an exploration. I have never taken anything at face value. My husband taught me to question. We had late night theological arguments. I'm not a stupid woman, Ms. Henderson. But even stupid people still have brains enough to think for themselves and pride enough not to be spoon-fed one particular way of looking at the world.

MYRA. Belief in God, Ms. Sprawley is as basic a thing as we have. And belief in a loving God – a God who *doesn't* punish people like your late husband – that's fundamental too. Tommy was telling the other children that there isn't a God and if there was, that he wasn't a very nice man. Can you imagine the position this puts us in? We've started hearing from some of the parents. One couple is getting ready to pull their son from the school if action isn't taken.

DEANNE. Pull the kid out and put him into some other little box somewhere else.

(DEANNE *gets up.*)

Thank you for opening my eyes, Ms. Henderson. I won't pull the fox and the grapes routine on you, because I actually *do* believe in your mission up to a point. I think we all need some degree of spirituality in our lives. That's why I argued with Tom to let Tommy go here – to give him a good spiritual foundation. But there are other ways – better ways, I think – to do that. Especially now that Tommy has become so fragile. Come on, Daddy. We're going now.

(HUCK *gets up.* DEANNE *and* HUCK *start out.* HUCK *stops. He turns to* MYRA.)

HUCK. I'd like to say something if I can.

(MYRA *consents with a nod.*)

I think my son-in-law is with God right now. That's what I believe. I believe that God don't push nobody away. Even folks that don't believe in him. If a man's got himself a good heart, why, that's enough for God. And my son-in-law had a good heart. He loved his pa, and he loved his ma when they walked this earth, and his wife – why, I pray thanks to the Lord every night that my baby found a good man like him. And he loved his little boy like nobody's business. See, it's about love, Ms. Henderson – about picking people up when they fall down and helping them to get going on their way again. And now my family has taken a bad turn. And I'm not gonna say what anybody ought to do or say when they been put in a place like this. All I see is the hurt in my grandboy's eyes. Because he's broken bad, Ms. Henderson. We're all broken, ma'am. Each and every one of us. And it ain't the time to stick to rules. Ain't no single rule gonna fix things. Only time and love. You don't have the time, Ms. Henderson, and you're coming up a mite bit short on the love. And that ain't right. But we'll make do. We'll get through this. Because we got God on our side, Ms. Henderson. I ain't too sure, though, just who *you folks* been praying to.

(to **DEANNE***)*

Come on, Pumpkin.

*(***HUCK** *and* **DEANNE** *walk out, leaving* **MYRA** *alone with her thoughts as lights fade out.)*

The Sixth Interview

VINCENT GAMPION
JULIANNA BUCHNER

(Lights come up on **VINCENT GAMPION** *sitting behind his desk.* **JULIANNA BUCHNER** *sits in the chair next to the desk.)*

JULIANNA. *(looking about the room)* I wasn't expecting an office.

VINCENT. Oh? What were you expecting?

JULIANNA. I don't know.

VINCENT. We'd meet in some alley? Or at the end of a darkened pier?

JULIANNA. Maybe your car.

VINCENT. Would you feel more comfortable if we went out to my car?

JULIANNA. No, I just – I've never done this before.

VINCENT. I'd be quite shocked if you had. Do you want coffee? I can have my secretary make us coffee.

JULIANNA. You have a secretary?

VINCENT. I run a legitimate business here, Ms. Buchner… in addition to my other, less publicized vocation.

JULIANNA. Oh.

VINCENT. Back to the coffee.

JULIANNA. No coffee. Thank you for asking. I just want to get this over with.

(pulling out a piece of paper)

I have some questions.

*(***VINCENT** *takes the piece of paper. He pulls out a cigarette lighter and sets it to flame.)*

VINCENT. Don't write things down, Ms. Buchner. In this business – my other less publicized line of work – we don't write things down.

JULIANNA. I'm sorry, I –

VINCENT. *(dropping the burnt paper into his ashtray)* Let me go first. That's generally how this works. I ask you some questions and then I decide if we are to proceed.

JULIANNA. All right.

VINCENT. You were told that the interview would go both ways. You were told this, am I right?

JULIANNA. Yes, you're right. I'm very nervous.

VINCENT. I have de-caf.

(She shakes her head.)

So.

(after a beat) Tell me what I don't know.

JULIANNA. You followed the case on the news, Mr. Gampion. You *know* why I'm here. You know what I *want.* What else do you need to know?

VINCENT. Who told you to come to me? Who referred you? I'm not listed in the Yellow Pages.

JULIANNA. My ex-brother-law Charlie. The one who called you.

VINCENT. Charlie didn't call me.

JULIANNA. He didn't?

VINCENT. That's not how this works. Charlie called somebody else who called somebody else. There are several degrees of separation here. For obvious reasons.

JULIANNA. I don't know how this works.

VINCENT. Of course you don't. So was there anyone else you talked to besides Charlie? About this. About what you wanted to do.

JULIANNA. Just Charlie.

VINCENT. Not even in passing. Not even in some off-handed way.

JULIANNA. People know my feelings on this. They also know –

(She stops herself.)

VINCENT. That what? That it would never be in your nature to seek out someone like me?

(JULIANNA *nods*.)

JULIANNA. *(after a beat)* But I'm not that person anymore. The person they think they know. Nobody, not even Bill, knows how I've changed.

VINCENT. And Bill. Your husband Bill. He doesn't know that you're doing this?

JULIANNA. I told you. I haven't talked to anybody else about this. Just Charlie.

VINCENT. But I'm sure you tell Bill everything.

JULIANNA. I didn't tell him about this.

VINCENT. Because he would never…

JULIANNA. He would never.

VINCENT. Where are you getting the money?

JULIANNA. My father left me some money.

VINCENT. That Bill doesn't know about.

JULIANNA. I've worked it all out. I've covered my tracks.

(beat)

Bill isn't like me. Bill just wants to get past this. He wants us to get our lives back – start to move forward again.

VINCENT. But you can't.

JULIANNA. No.

(beat)

I need closure. I can't get closure. Not while Towler is still out there. Still free.

VINCENT. Did you say anything to the D.A.? After the acquittal. Did you say anything to the D.A. that would make him think you might be thinking of taking the law into your own hands?

JULIANNA. No. I called him…*names*. And the police officers who botched the case. I called them vile names and I cried. There were cameras there. I made a scene in the

courtroom. You probably saw it on TV. I did everything
that any other mother in my situation would have
done. But I made no threats. I didn't tip my hand.
Even as the thought came to me in that moment. That
it *wasn't* over. Even as I stood sobbing into the arms of
my ineffectual husband. I vowed that this wasn't over.
Not by a long shot. That something would be done to
the man who did this to my daughter.

VINCENT. And that's when you got the idea to talk to your
ex-brother-in-law Charlie.

JULIANNA. He'd just been released from prison a few
months ago. I knew that he'd know people.

VINCENT. People like me.

JULIANNA. And Teresa happened to mention where I could
find him.

VINCENT. You didn't ask her?

JULIANNA. You're very thorough. No. I didn't ask her. It
just came out. I read this as a sign that I should do this.

VINCENT. Can I ask about your daughter?

JULIANNA. Why?

VINCENT. I'm curious. I followed the case like everybody
else.

JULIANNA. There's one more surgery scheduled for next
month. We're praying it's the last.

VINCENT. How is she holding up?

JULIANNA. You really want to know? You kill people for a
living. You're a hired contract-killer, and you actually
care whether my six-year-old daughter is ever going to
be whole again?

VINCENT. My specialty is retributive killings, Ms. Buchner.
Righteous vigilante hits. Maybe your ex-brother-in-law
didn't tell you. As a rule, I terminate only certain kinds
of people – the kinds of people whose deaths don't
keep me up at night.

JULIANNA. You sound like a TV show.

VINCENT. I don't enjoy killing people, Ms. Buchner. As a
rule. But there's a certain lift you get when the person

has it coming. You know that the most that Towler could have gotten for the brutal rape of your daughter, Ms. Buchner, was life imprisonment. Under the best of circumstances in this state. You must also know that in this particular case you're asking me to go beyond what the law – even if it had been working properly – would have doled out.

JULIANNA. I want him dead. He had every intention of killing my daughter. It wasn't a sudden pang of conscience that stopped him. It was that janitor showing up before he'd finished her off.

VINCENT. Yes. I know the case.

JULIANNA. So what else is it you need to know?

VINCENT. Charlie told you my price.

JULIANNA. I can pay it.

VINCENT. Then we're set on this end. Now is there anything you need to find out about *me?*

JULIANNA. I'd like to know how you plan to do it.

VINCENT. Fair question. I haven't worked out the details yet.

JULIANNA. I want him to suffer. He'll never suffer as much as my daughter did, but I want you to do your best.

VINCENT. I'm not going to torture him.

JULIANNA. *I* would.

VINCENT. You would?

JULIANNA. If I could.

VINCENT. I'll take him out. Cleanly and efficiently. He isn't going to do this to anybody else's little girl.

JULIANNA. That isn't enough.

VINCENT. You want to punish him.

JULIANNA. Yes.

(*beat*)

Do you have children, Mr. Gampion?

VINCENT. Yes. He's grown. I haven't seen him in years.

JULIANNA. So you don't know, then.

VINCENT. I do know. I understand.

JULIANNA. You'll never know. I'm going to be sick. I have to go.

(She gets up.)

VINCENT. I have one last question of my own.

(She doesn't move.)

Please.

(She sits back down.)

I have to know if there is any chance – between now and when I make the hit – any time *after* I make the hit – if there's any chance you'll come to think differently about this. Any chance that guilt will set in, that you'll tell someone. That you'll confess it to your priest...

JULIANNA. I'm Presbyterian.

VINCENT. Because it can't happen. Because if it *does* happens I will have no choice but to view it as a violation of our agreement.

JULIANNA. And what?

VINCENT. Take a guess, Ms. Buchner. Take a guess at what I will be compelled to do.

JULIANNA. *(without levity)* Now you're talking like a hit man. How do I get the money to you?

VINCENT. We'll work that out later. I'll be in touch with Charlie through channels.

(She gets up.)

JULIANNA. So that's it.

VINCENT. That's about it.

JULIANNA. I walk out of that door and it happens.

VINCENT. At some point. Maybe this week. Maybe next month. It'll happen. Don't call me. Don't ever come back here. Don't get impatient. I honor all of my contracts.

JULIANNA. What I mean is...

VINCENT. Yes, I know what you mean, Ms. Buchner. You walk out that door and a man dies. The man who brutally raped and disfigured your daughter. That man pays for his crime Old Testament style. I am the instrument, Ms. Buchner. But you wrote the check. You pulled the switch. You have to be able to live with that. Can you live with that?

JULIANNA. It's all I've thought about since he walked out of that courtroom. I wake up in the middle of the night wanting him dead. I stand in the produce section of Krogers wanting him dead. I sit at green traffic lights with people blaring their horns and I want him dead. I've never wanted anything so much in my life. Except...

VINCENT. Except for what, Ms. Buchner?

JULIANNA. To be dead myself. But I have to stay alive. I have to nurse Kimmie back to health. I have to be her mommy. There is one other thing. One other thing, Mr. Gampion, that I wish for more. It's an impossible wish: that this should never have happened. That I should have Kimmie back the way it was before. I wish to turn back the clock, Mr. Gampion. But I can't. And I can't go out some night and drive my car off an overpass. So I do the only thing I *can* do: I ask you to end the life of the man who tried to end my daughter's life, and who ended up destroying it nonetheless. That is what I can do. I don't care what God thinks. I don't care what the Bible says. I don't care what compassion requires. I care nothing about any of those things. Kill him, Mr. Gampion. Do it slow or do it quick. Do it however you see fit. And know that I will never change my mind. It won't put Kimmie back the way she was. It won't put Bill and me back the way we were. But I want it done. Now *I* get to be the criminal. Now it's *my* turn. Goodbye Mr. Gampion.

(She exits. Lights slowly fade out.)

The Seventh Interview

MS. DOMANIAN
ABEL MARCH
BRITTNEY FLETCHER

*(Lights come up on **MS. DOMANIAN**, dressed in her cleaning woman's uniform. A big carry-all bag rests at her feet. She sits behind a desk, her arms folded in a defensive posture. **ABEL MARCH** stands over her. Upon the desk are several items of note: a small opened bag of potato chips, several issues of Car and Driver magazine, three neckties of different colors. **ABEL** holds in his hand a wad of money, which he counts out upon the desk.)*

ABEL. Fifty, one-hundred, one-fifty, one-seventy, one-ninety, two-ten, two-eleven, two-twelve, two- thirteen, two-eighteen.

*(glaring at **MS. DOMANIAN**)*

Where's the rest of it?

*(**MS. DOMANIAN** makes an expansive "I don't know" gesture with her hands.)*

ABEL. There was two-hundred-and-fifty dollars in this desk. Not two-eighteen. What's your name?

MS. DOMANIAN. *(with a non-specific Eastern European accent)* My name it is Domanian.

ABEL. Doe what?

MS. DOMANIAN. I am Ms. Domanian.

ABEL. Ms. Domanian: where's the other thirty-two dollars? Have you already stashed it in your bag?

MS. DOMANIAN. Is not in my bag. I have the lipstick in my bag and the brush for the hair and the eyelash stick. And I have the cleaning wipes in my bag and the spray that squirts to clean the wood.

ABEL. *(rolling his eyes)* Thank you for the inventory.

MS. DOMANIAN. I must go home, Mr. March. I must go to my house.

(She starts to rise from the chair.)

ABEL. *(shaking his head)* Uh uh.

(He pushes her back down.)

I have more questions. How long have you been going through my drawers after hours?

MS. DOMANIAN. I do not go through the drawers.

ABEL. They were wide open when I walked in here. What were you doing? Airing them out?

MS. DOMANIAN. I did not do this thing.

ABEL. So who 'did this thing', huh? Who – if not you – opened up all these drawers and pulled all of this – this *stuff* out onto my desk?

(pointing to the stuff piled on the desk)

And the top drawer – the drawer where I keep the petty cash – is also open. It was closed. It was locked. It is now unlocked and noticeably open. Who did all of this, Ms. Domanian, if you not you?

MS. DOMANIAN. I do not know. I must go to my house. My sister come with the childrens.

ABEL. You're not going home until I get some answers.

MS. DOMANIAN. But is Christmas Eve and my sister Ivanka – she come with the childrens.

ABEL. Last week I discovered one-hundred-fifty dollars missing from my desk. From the locked drawer. Did you take it? Did you take the seventy-five dollars that was missing the week before? What do you do, Ms. Domanian – do you pick the lock? Is that one of the things they teach you in your part of the world?

MS. DOMANIAN. I do not look through your drawers, Mr. March. I do not take your money.

ABEL. So how were the potato chips?

MS. DOMANIAN. Wha?

ABEL. My bag of potato chips. You obviously ate my potato chips. I left the bag unopened in the second drawer. Note that the bag is no longer in the second drawer. It lies crumpled and empty right here on the top of my desk. And note as well, Ms. Domanian, that there are potato chip crumbs on your chin.

(**MS. DOMANIAN** *quickly brushes crumbs from her chin.*)

MS. **DOMANIAN**. This is not potato chip crumbles. This is Frito crumbles. I have Frito crispies for my dinner.

ABEL. *(picking up the magazines)*

Do you read *Car and Driver* magazine, Ms. Domanian? Is this periodical of some special interest to you? What were you going to do with my neckties, Ms. Domanian?

(picking up the neckties)

Sell them on the street? You won't get much for them, but we can dream can't we?

MS. **DOMANIAN**. They pretty.

ABEL. I beg your pardon?

MS. **DOMANIAN**. They pretty ties. Who buy them? Your wife? She buy them?

ABEL. Keep my wife out of this. You, Ms. Domanian, are a thief. You have been stealing from me for the last two months. I assume that this is how long you've been cleaning my office. Am I right, Ms. Domanian? Have you been stealing from me since you first joined the night crew? Where *is* the rest of your cleaning crew, by the way?

MS. **DOMANIAN**. They go home. Is Christmas Eve.

ABEL. But you thought you'd stay behind – see what kind of little Christmas present Mr. March had waiting for you in his *locked* top drawer. But I foiled your plan, didn't I? Tonight I was lying in wait to catch you red-handed.

MS. **DOMANIAN**. My hands they are not red.

ABEL. It's a figure of speech. I don't know what I'm going to do with you.

MS. **DOMANIAN**. I go to my house.

ABEL. Yes, I know. The "childrens" are coming. Look, you don't get off the hook because it's Christmas. You don't come over to this country and steal from people. That's not the way it works.

MS. DOMANIAN. I do not steal from you.

ABEL. So what were you intending to do? Pay back all the money with interest? What rate were you going to give yourself? Let me hear your terms.

MS. DOMANIAN. I do not understand – you speak too quickly.

ABEL. Then I'll speak slowly. The words on the statue do not say "Give me your tired and your poor and your huddled *thieving* masses. That's not what the words say, Ms. Domanian.

(shifting gears)

This is pointless. Your interrogation is over. I'm going to let you go home. Enjoy your Christmas. But don't bother reporting to work on Monday night. Because there won't be a job waiting for you. I'm going to talk to your employer. I plan to make a list of all the things that have gone missing, tally up how much money has disappeared from petty cash.

(takes out his cell phone)

And I have the proof. Right here. Caught in the act.

(looks at the picture on the phone)

If that doesn't look like the face of a guilty woman, then I don't know what does.

*(He shows the picture to **MS. DOMANIAN**.)*

MS. DOMANIAN. My hair in that picture: is a mess.

(arranging her hair a little)

You take another one.

ABEL. That would defeat the purpose.

MS. DOMANIAN. I bring back all the money.

ABEL. So you admit it.

MS. DOMANIAN. I bring back all the money I take. And the handkerchiefs and the Little Debbie cakes.

ABEL. No, Ms. Domanian. That will not suffice. You are a thief. A thief in the night. And you must be taught that certain actions have consequences.

MS. DOMANIAN. Consee –

ABEL. *Quences*, Ms. Domanian.

MS. DOMANIAN. Is Christmas Eve.

ABEL. Call me Scrooge. No I'm not Scrooge. I am a decent, law-abiding citizen. *I* don't break the law. I work hard for my family. I've earned everything I've ever gotten, Ms. Domanian. Now there's a lesson –

(The cell phone in **ABEL***'s hand RINGS.)*

There's a lesson you have yet to learn.

(into phone)

Hi.

(listens)

Soon.

(listens)

Maybe an hour. I don't know.

(turning his back to **MS. DOMANIAN** *for more privacy)*

You know it's the last chance I'll have to be with my brother before he flies back to Germany.

(listens)

I'm not the problem here, Selena. It's you and Robert who don't get along. Otherwise I wouldn't have to be visiting with my kid brother on Christmas Eve all by myself. So I'll be home when I get home, okay? All right?

(He listens. A look of extreme uneasiness suddenly comes over his face.)

What do you mean?

(He listens.)

I mean, I thought you and Robert hated each other's – so what are you doing at his house? Why are you making merry with Robert and Gloria when you said – ?

(listens, improvising an alibi)

I'm driving around. In the car, Selena. I'm driving around because I need to be alone for a while. I hate Christmas. You know how much I hate Christmas.

(listens)

All right. Okay.

(He hangs up.)

Damn.

(He turns to **MS. DOMANIAN**.*)*

Did you hear any of that?

MS. DOMANIAN. No.

ABEL. Of course you did. I was forced to lie to my wife about my whereabouts. I lied because I didn't want her to know that I've been sitting in the car in that freezing parking lot for the last two hours like a crazy man waiting for the light to come on up here and you to start robbing me.

MS. DOMANIAN. I give it all back.

ABEL. This isn't good. Oh God.

MS. DOMANIAN. I make you pretty plate. I paint the chicken on it.

ABEL. Huh?

MS. DOMANIAN. I paint you a pretty plate with the chicken. It make you smile.

ABEL. What the hell are you talking about?

(beat, largely to himself)

I'm suffocating here. She's like that – that – what's that sea bird?

MS. DOMANIAN. Penguin?

ABEL. No. The one the sailors – albatross. She's like an albatross around my neck.

MS. DOMANIAN. Who?

ABEL. My ball and chain. I can't divorce her. Her father would fire me. I like my job...when people aren't taking things from my desk. Do you know that you leave your scent, Ms. Domanian? You leave the scent of whatever that Slavic perfume is you wear. I come in on Tuesday and Friday mornings and I can still smell it. That's how I knew. That's when I got suspicious. Go home to your family, Ms. Domanian. Merry Christmas. I won't call your employer. My Christmas present. But if you ever so much as crack open one of these drawers in the future –

MS. DOMANIAN. Thank you, Mr. March. You are a good man and God bless you and God bless your family.

(**MS. DOMANIAN** *shakes hands with* **ABEL**. *The two are still shaking hands,* **MS. DOMANIAN** *most effusively, when* **BRITTNEY FLETCHER** *enters.*)

BRITTNEY. (*to* **ABEL**) What are you doing? I'm freezing my buns off down there.

ABEL. (*thrown for a moment by her sudden appearance*) I'm done here. Let's go.

BRITTNEY. I'm cold. Give me a minute to warm up. Oh look. Potato chips.

MS. DOMANIAN. No potato chips. All gone. I have Fritos in my bag.

BRITTNEY. I like Fritos.

(*to* **ABEL**)

I'm starving, Abel. You said we'd be eating dinner hours ago. You're ruining my Christmas Eve.

(**MS. DOMANIAN** *pulls a bag of Fritos from her bag. The two women begin to munch the chips.*)

BRITTNEY. (*to* **MS. DOMANIAN**, *obscenely curious*) So did he catch you in the act? Did he grill you? Did he make you quake in your boots?

MS. DOMANIAN. *(apparently not quite sure how to respond)* I do not wear boots.

ABEL. Ms. Domanian and I have come to an understanding. She admitted to the thefts and will be returning all of the money.

BRITTNEY. She isn't going to jail?

(to MS. DOMANIAN, regarding the Fritos)

Do you have any dip?

ABEL. *(not giving MS. DOMANIAN a chance to answer)* She isn't going to jail. Are you warmed up yet?

(taking her by the arm to pull her to the side for a quick sotto voce)

Selena called. She's drinking eggnog with my alibi. I have to take you home.

BRITTNEY. That's it? That's Christmas Eve? I had a better Christmas Eve the night the reform school burned down.

ABEL. Please don't raise your voice.

BRITTNEY. I'm sick of this, Abel. You don't divorce her but you don't do nothing for me to make up for it.

ABEL. I thought we had a nice –

BRITTNEY. We sat in a car, Abel – for over an hour – while you waited for this light to come on. Then you couldn't wait to get up here. It's like *she's* the one you're having the affair with.

ABEL. *(apparently noticing that MS. DOMANIAN isn't leaving)* Go home, Ms. Domanian. Merry Christmas.

(MS. DOMANIAN still doesn't leave. Instead, she eases back down into ABEL's chair.)

(to BRITTNEY) Do you want it to be over, Brittney? Because it isn't much fun for me either these days. I think Selena's getting suspicious. I don't know that for sure, but I know that even though she hates Robert's guts, something told her to go over there tonight – to find out if what I was telling her was true. And guess what, Brittney? It wasn't true. She caught me in a flat-out lie about my whereabouts. I'm a liar, Brittney. Ms. Domanian's a thief – GO HOME, MS. DOMANIAN – and you're an ex-stripper with a very unsympathetic nature – and me, I'm a liar.

BRITTNEY. I do so have a sympathetic nature! I just can't see you anymore.

ABEL. Look, I can make this up to you.

BRITTNEY. Promises, promises. Look, sugar, here's the thing: I just don't like you very much. I mean – you've been pretty nice to me overall – the things you give me and how much you wanted to spend Christmas Eve with me, which was very sweet, before, you know, it all went down the toilet. I thought, well, I could learn to love this man. But I can't. No, baby, I can't. You're really screwed up, Abel. You sat down there poised on the seat like a crazy man and why? Because you wanted to ambush your building's cleaning lady. That's a little sick in my book. Now why would you want to do that?

ABEL. She was stealing from me.

BRITTNEY. So what? I've stolen from plenty of people. When things were bad. I'm not saying it's right. I'm just saying that sometimes people have to do things. But I don't want to do *this* anymore. And I could care less whether you go back to your wife or not, so it's not about that. It's just about: you're messed up Abel. And I don't need one more messed up person in my life. Give me twenty for a cab and let's say goodbye.

ABEL. *(in a slight state of shock)* Twenty.

(He opens his wallet and takes out a couple of small bills. Helplessly.)

I don't think I –

MS. DOMANIAN. *(waving a twenty-dollar bill)* I have a twenty bill from the desk!

*(**BRITTNEY** goes to her and takes it.)*

BRITTNEY. *(to* **MS. DOMANIAN***)* Thank you. And thanks for dinner.

(She offers **ABEL** *an angry scowl as she exits. There follows a lengthy silence, with* **ABEL** *remaining where he is, his back still turned to* **MS. DOMANIAN***.)*

ABEL. *(still without turning around)* What are you still doing here, Ms. Domanian?

MS. DOMANIAN. You have the affair with the young woman?

ABEL. No. We were just friends. I was giving her a ride home.

MS. DOMANIAN. No, no. You have the affair with the young woman while your wife she waits for you. She doesn't know, does she? She doesn't know you have the affair with the young woman?

ABEL. *(defeated, deflated)* It doesn't matter.

MS. DOMANIAN. Of course it matter.

ABEL. She'll never know. I'll fix it. Do what I can to keep it from her. This is what I do. To keep up this sham of a marriage. I've gotten very good at it.

MS. DOMANIAN. You not so good maybe this time?

ABEL. Brittney won't say anything. That isn't her style.

MS. DOMANIAN. No, but *I* say something.

ABEL. *(now turning)* Say something to who?

MS. DOMANIAN. To your wife. To your Selena. I will tell her about the Brittanee.

ABEL. Why would you do that?

MS. DOMANIAN. Is a color word.

ABEL. A color word? What are you talking about?

MS. DOMANIAN. Black. Yes.

ABEL. Black what?

MS. DOMANIAN. Black mail.

ABEL. You're proposing to blackmail me?

MS. DOMANIAN. I *will* blackmail you. This is what I will do.

ABEL. But I don't understand. I let you off the hook. I'm not reporting you.

MS. DOMANIAN. Is not about that. I need the money.

ABEL. Everybody needs money. Times are tough. But people aren't all going around blackmailing each other.

MS. DOMANIAN. Is easy thing for me to do. You have the affair with the young woman. If I tell your wife, she tell her father and he take your job away. But you give me money and I will not tell your wife. Is very easy thing.

ABEL. Ms. Domanian, have you no sense of decency?

MS. DOMANIAN. *(shrugging)* I need money.

ABEL. For what? You having a lean Christmas this year? I get it, I get it. All right, here's what we'll do: we'll go out – you and me, right now and we'll – what's open at this hour? Walmart? Target? I'll take you to whatever store is still open and I'll do the Santa thing and then you don't have to blackmail me. How much were you going to ask for?

MS. DOMANIAN. Ten-thousand-four-hundred-and-fifty-seven dollars.

ABEL. *(nonplussed)* I beg your –

MS. DOMANIAN. Ten-thousand-four-hundred-and-fifty-seven-dollars to bring over my brother Pavel and his wife Lumenka and their four children, and Lumenka's father and his iron lung. And there is one goat and one pig that must not be left behind.

ABEL. You're joking.

(She shakes her head.)

I don't have that kind of money.

MS. DOMANIAN. Then I tell your wife.

ABEL. Then I will have you fired.

MS. DOMANIAN. And you will be fired as well. I have seen the father of your wife. He is not so nice a man.

ABEL. This is ridiculous.

MS. DOMANIAN. My brother now he is poor man. I was poor too. But now I am in the richest country in the world and I have a job cleaning people's offices.

ABEL. And cleaning out their desks.

MS. DOMANIAN. *(ignoring this)* And there are times that I forget the ones I lost in the war. I remember them, yes, but sometimes I do not have to remember them so that it tears so much my heart. Times like tonight when I hear the Christmas music come from out in the big room there and everyone humming and so, so – what is the Christmas word?

ABEL. Jolly.

MS. DOMANIAN. Yes! And I sit here and eat the chocolate cakes that the little girl with the hat sells – the Littlest Debbie – which I find in your desk. And I sit here and count up the money that will bring my brother Pavel to me, for it has been eight years since I have seen him. And there are two new babies I have not yet seen. And I want them here in this country where I can make them all safe and the bad memories – they're not so much with us here.

ABEL. You feel safe here.

MS. DOMANIAN. Listen.

ABEL. What?

MS. DOMANIAN. There is a little singing I hear out of window. Christmas singing. And little bells. There are no bombs here.

*(**ABEL** collapses into a chair.)*

ABEL. I'll give you some money. I can't give you ten thousand. But I'll try to help you as best as I can. Now what am I going to do about my marriage?

MS. DOMANIAN. The marriage bad?

ABEL. Yes, Ms. Domanian. The marriage very bad. Who am I fooling? She knows. I know she knows. She knows I've been screwing around on her. She knows I don't love her. She knows that I'm trapped in a marriage that doesn't make me happy. And I know that she doesn't love *me*. But Selena would die before she admitted to the world that our marriage is a failure. I don't know why I'm telling you this. You probably aren't getting half of what I'm saying.

MS. DOMANIAN. I get it. I get it. Mr. March?

ABEL. Yeah?

MS. DOMANIAN. I no longer wish to blackmail you.

ABEL. *(with a sarcastic bite)* Thank you. Merry Christmas.

MS. DOMANIAN. Is not right. Is not a country to live happy life by stealing and making the black mail.

ABEL. Thank you, Ms. Domanian. That was a gesture perfect for the season.

MS. DOMANIAN. You help me by not taking my job away. I wish that I could help you, but I cannot. I do not know a marriage with no love. I loved my husband very much.

ABEL. Where is he? Is he gone?

MS. DOMANIAN. Died in the war. Died in a very bad way. Many of my family die. I lost – I lost many peoples.

ABEL. I'm sorry.

MS. DOMANIAN. I am here now. Is better. My sister is here now. We will bring my brother too.

ABEL. And all his kith and kin, yes, Ms. Domanian, we'll work on that.

MS. DOMANIAN. Thank you.

ABEL. Please go home, Ms. Domanian. Go to your sister.

*(**MS. DOMANIAN** nods. She gets up from the chair and stops beside **ABEL**. She reaches out her hand and takes his.)*

MS. DOMANIAN. You smile now. Is soon Christmas.

*(**ABEL** nods, but without smiling. **MS. DOMANIAN** goes. **ABEL** sits for a moment, then goes to the desk and begins to return all of its emptied contents back into their respective drawers. His eyes fall on something that we don't for a moment see. Then slowly he pulls it up and holds it in front of him. It is a large decorative plate with*

a chicken hand-painted upon it. He laughs warmly.
Apostrophic to **MS. DOMANIAN***:)*

And Happy New Year, Ms. Domanian. Happy New Year,
God willing, to us both.

(Lights fade out.)

End of Play

SAMUEL FRENCH STAFF

Nate Collins
President

Ken Dingledine
Director of Operations,
Vice President

Bruce Lazarus
Executive Director,
General Counsel

Rita Maté
Director of Finance

ACCOUNTING

Lori Thimsen | Director of Licensing Compliance
Nehal Kumar | Senior Accounting Associate
Charles Graytok | Accounting and Finance Manager
Glenn Halcomb | Royalty Administration
Jessica Zheng | Accounts Receivable
Andy Lian | Accounts Payable
Charlie Sou | Accounting Associate
Joann Mannello | Orders Administrator

BUSINESS AFFAIRS

Caitlin Bartow | Assistant to the Executive Director

CORPORATE COMMUNICATIONS

Abbie Van Nostrand | Director of Corporate
Communications

CUSTOMER SERVICE AND LICENSING

Brad Lohrenz | Director of Licensing Development
Laura Lindson | Licensing Services Manager
Kim Rogers | Theatrical Specialist
Matthew Akers | Theatrical Specialist
Ashley Byrne | Theatrical Specialist
Jennifer Carter | Theatrical Specialist
Annette Storckman | Theatrical Specialist
Julia Izumi | Theatrical Specialist
Sarah Weber | Theatrical Specialist
Nicholas Dawson | Theatrical Specialist
David Kimple | Theatrical Specialist
Ryan McLeod | Theatrical Specialist

EDITORIAL

Amy Rose Marsh | Literary Manager
Ben Coleman | Literary Associate

MARKETING

Ryan Pointer | Marketing Manager
Courtney Kochuba | Marketing Associate
Chris Kam | Marketing Associate

PUBLICATIONS AND PRODUCT DEVELOPMENT

Joe Ferreira | Product Development Manager
David Geer | Publications Manager
Charlyn Brea | Publications Associate
Tyler Mullen | Publications Associate
Derek P. Hassler | Musical Products Coordinator
Zachary Orts | Musical Materials Coordinator

OPERATIONS

Casey McLain | Operations Supervisor
Elizabeth Minski | Office Coordinator, Reception
Coryn Carson | Office Coordinator, Reception

SAMUEL FRENCH BOOKSHOP (LOS ANGELES)

Joyce Mehess | Bookstore Manager
Cory DeLair | Bookstore Buyer
Kristen Springer | Customer Service Manager
Tim Coultas | Bookstore Associate
Bryan Jansyn | Bookstore Associate
Alfred Contreras | Shipping & Receiving

LONDON OFFICE

Anne-Marie Ashman | Accounts Assistant
Felicity Barks | Rights & Contracts Associate
Steve Blacker | Bookshop Associate
David Bray | Customer Services Associate
Robert Cooke | Assistant Buyer
Stephanie Dawson | Amateur Licensing Associate
Simon Ellison | Retail Sales Manager
Robert Hamilton | Amateur Licensing Associate
Peter Langdon | Marketing Manager
Louise Mappley | Amateur Licensing Associate
James Nicolau | Despatch Associate
Emma Anacootee-Parmar | Production/Editorial
Controller
Martin Phillips | Librarian
Panos Panayi | Company Accountant
Zubayed Rahman | Despatch Associate
Steve Sanderson | Royalty Administration Supervisor
Douglas Schatz | Acting Executive Director
Roger Sheppard | I.T. Manager
Debbie Simmons | Licensing Sales Team Leader
Peter Smith | Amateur Licensing Associate
Garry Spratley | Customer Service Manager
David Webster | UK Operations Director
Sarah Wolf | Rights Director